Child of Fire

Child of Fire

SCOTT O'DELL

Houghton Mifflin Company Boston

Library of Congress Cataloging in Publication Data

O'Dell, Scott, 1903–
Child of fire.

SUMMARY: A parole officer relates his efforts to
keep the violence and heroics of two young Chicanos
under control.
[1. Mexicans in the United States — Fiction]
I. Title.
PZ7.0237Ch   [Fic]   74–8718
ISBN 0–395–19496–2

To Austin and Mary K. and Walter
Fellow Workers in the Vineyard

Child of Fire

1

It was a bad day for the bullfights.

There was a strong wind blowing — one of those santanas that come down from the high desert country through the Chocolate Mountains and the Lagunas. The wind was hot and dry and it picked up dust and swirled it around in the bullring. The dust was so thick that sometimes you couldn't see from one side of the ring to the other.

They should have called the fights off. But if they had, the crowd would have taken the place apart board by board and burned it all in a big bonfire in the center of the plaza.

It would have been all right with me. I wouldn't miss the fights at all. I go down to Tijuana about once a month when I want to see Lieutenant Morales on business. It's always on a Sunday because Morales is busy during the week chasing smugglers, looking for reds and marijuana. Morales is a bullfight fan — an aficionado as they say in Spanish — and when I am down there on Sunday I go along with him to the fights.

The reason for the crowd on this dusty afternoon was a mano a mano between El Gato, the Spanish matador, and El Burrito, the most popular of the young Mexican matadors.

If you don't know about bullfighting, mano a mano is a contest between two matadors. Usually there are three. Each takes a turn at killing a bull. But in the mano a mano, the two matadors compete against one another. The competition spurs the matador into taking chances on getting himself killed that he wouldn't take otherwise. This brings the crowds.

The fights started slow. The first bull was small. The board where they chalk up the weights showed that he weighed 850 pounds. But he didn't weigh more than 700 and the crowd knew it. Before El Gato had made the first pass with his cape the catcalls began.

"*Vaya! Torito va a su casa.* Little bull go home."

"He is somebody's sister."

"A grandmother!"

Lieutenant Morales turned and looked at me. He had a fat nose and a heavy chin and very white teeth. "It is a robust rat," he said softly, as if he were telling me a secret. "We have among us a corpulent rat."

The bull stood in front of the toril. He had come through it into the plaza de toros and it was now closed behind him. He looked at the closed gate and then around at the crowd and then at one of the matador's attendants who was tripping across the ring toward him. He seemed lost, standing in the bright sun with the hot wind whipping at his tail. His name was Victoriano but he was timid. A timid bull can be a dangerous bull. The attendant approached him carefully, ready to run.

Victoriano put his head down. For a while it seemed as if he might charge. Instead he began to paw the earth. It had just been watered down but the wind had dried it out already and a cloud of dust rose and blew across the arena. Bulls that paw the earth are usually cowards.

"It is a bad beginning," Morales said. "That one comes from an untrustworthy source. The Double O ranch in Hermosillo. The rest of the bulls likewise come from Double O. We waste the afternoon I think, perhaps."

"It doesn't look good," I said.

"I think we should go to La Paloma and have one of their cool beers," Morales said.

As if his words were a signal, the little gray bull stopped pawing the earth. He raised his head and pricked his ears. He located the attendant who had come to a halt about ten steps in front of him, then charged.

Fighting bulls are very fast. They can outrun a horse, even a polo pony for a distance of fifty feet. And distances in a bullring are measured in feet, in inches, even in fractions of an inch.

The attendant held the muleta in his right hand, at arm's length. At first he must have thought that he had centered the bull's attention on the red cloth. But in an instant he saw that it was not charging the cape. The bull was charging straight toward him and, unless he moved, he would be gored. He dropped the muleta and fled. Zigzagging, which is the best way to flee from a bull, he reached the wooden barrier and scrambled over.

There was a murmur of disapproval from the crowd, but only a murmur. An attendant is not a matador. He is not supposed to risk his neck. His job is to try out the bull — to show the matador what kind of an animal he is dealing with.

It was an exciting moment. The bull charging when he wasn't expected to. The attendant scrambling for his life over the high barrera, leaving behind his hat and one scarlet shoe.

But the little bull didn't last long. Lieutenant Morales gave him a lot of advice and shouted insults at the Spanish matador, but Victoriano died with the first sword thrust. He sprawled over on his back with his feet in the air like a child's toy, and the horses trotted in and two men tied a chain around his horns and dragged him briskly away.

He left a smooth trail across the earth where they had dragged him across the arena and out the gate. Looking at the trail and the blood, I said to Morales, "Why don't they put the dead bulls in a cart and take them away?"

Lieutenant Morales smiled, showing his white teeth. He always smiled when he didn't like something.

"Who is going to lift a dead bull into a cart?" he asked.

"The ones who kill the bull," I said.

"That would require the matador and the picador and two banderilleros and the mono and four attendants," Morales said, still smiling. "They would spend all the time just lifting the bulls and carting the bulls away. Then there would be no more bullfights, Señor."

"Good," is what I felt like saying. But I didn't say it. I said, "Have you ever run into a kid by the name of Ernesto de la Sierra?"

"That name I have never heard. Not in my life and I have fifty-two years."

"He's called Ernie."

"Ernie, yes. Many Ernies. A hundred Ernies."

"Ernie Sierra," I said.

While Morales tumbled the name over in his mind, I pulled out a picture I had taken from our files. It showed a boy about sixteen with a Prince Valiant haircut. He was dressed in a white pullover sweater with an insignia of an owl across the chest.

5

Lieutenant Morales glanced at the picture, then shook his head.

"They all look alike, these Chicanos," Morales said. "Up there in the U.S.A. you must possess a factory. Some place you stamp them out like automobile fenders. One after the other. All the same size and shape. You are very clever, you Anglos."

"This one is different," I said.

"This one is not a stealer of hubcaps, which he brings to Tijuana and sells for beer, with which he gets himself *mucho borracho* and gives us *mucho* trouble?"

"No, it's not that," I said. "But I'm not sure what it is. Sierra is a juvenile. I've had him for a couple of months. He reports in on time every week. He's the sullen type but he's given me no trouble. Simpson thinks he's stealing cars around San Diego and trading them down here for pills."

"Pills are not your department," Morales said.

"Not exactly. But Ernie Sierra's my ward. Whatever he does, it's my business."

Officially it really wasn't my business, but unofficially, if Sierra was stealing cars and buying pills, I wanted to know. They have a new rule in the Mar Vista Police Department that I don't like. All narcotic violations, whether they're real or suspected, adult or juvenile, are now in a special department. And in the charge of Lieutenant Simpson. I don't like this new rule and,

6

to be truthful about it, I don't like Simpson either.

"Forgive me if I am wrong," Morales said, "but you are getting into trouble with the pill business. Stay far away. *Muy lejos.* Permit him to have the big headache. He possesses a big head and he can accommodate a big headache."

"I'll appreciate it if you don't say anything to Simpson."

"Nothing to Simpson. *Nada,*" Morales said. "I understand this thing between you and Simpson. And I have my eye out for Sierra. Do I keep his photograph? No? Well, I have him in mind. Right here." He tapped his forehead with one finger.

"You might take a look at your files tomorrow."

"Tonight, Señor, I take a look."

"Call me in the morning if you find anything."

"Sure enough, Señor."

"And I will appreciate it if you say nothing to Simpson."

"*Nada.*"

I could depend upon Morales. I had asked little favors from him before and he had always come through. I knew that he would ask a big favor of me someday — twice as big as all the little favors. And it would have to do with money. A big mordida. But that was the way things worked south of the border.

7

2

The next two bulls did no better than Victoriano. But the fourth bull caused trouble.

The bull was named Cuerno Corvo, Crooked Horn, because of a left horn that slanted out at the tip. The Spanish matador didn't like the looks of the horn. He handled the bull with great care and turned him over to the Mexican matador after two brief flourishes with the cape. The crowd was disappointed. It gave out a burst of insults that sounded like an explosion, and a couple of cushions went sailing into the ring.

El Gato paid no attention to the insults or the cushions. He went over and stood against the barrera. The wind had died down a little but it was still very hot. He looked uncomfortable in his cotton stockings and his tight silk pants and the red sash wound around his stomach and the stiff jacket decorated with heavy gold. He mopped his face, watching while the Mexican matador experimented with the crooked horn.

El Burrito caped the bull out of the center of the ring. He drew him step by step toward the picador, who sat on his horse and waited with his steel-tipped pike pole.

At last the bull spied the horseman, gathered himself, and charged. He lowered his head and buried his horns in the horse, lifting him off the ground — all four feet at once — and flung him against the wooden barrier. The picador's wide, low-crowned hat with a pompom on the side, flew off and the wind carried it away.

Before he and the horse were flung against the wall, the picador jabbed the steel tip of his pike pole into the bull's shoulders, just back of the head, and put all of his weight against it.

Leaning hard on his long steel-tipped pole, the picador punished the bull. When El Burrito, the Mexican, saw that the bull had been punished enough, he stepped in with his cape and lured the bull away from the horse.

With the heart-shaped muleta held in both hands and his feet together, but the left foot slightly advanced, he led the bull past him very slowly in a pretty Veronica, which is a figure, a pass named after Saint Veronica who held the napkin in both her hands and wiped the face of Christ. Then he shifted his body ever so little, and putting his right foot slightly ahead, he brought the bull back, passing it close to his waist, and as the bull followed the cape he raised it, shifted his feet again, and again brought the bull by. So close this time that a horn tore off one of the gold rosettes on his jacket.

The crowd cheered. They showered the ring with hats and flowers and purses. El Burrito's attendants went around and picked up everything but the flowers and tossed them back into the crowd. El Burrito took one of the roses and fastened it to his jacket, bowed, and turned the bull over to El Gato for the third part of the fight.

Usually the banderilleros set the slender harpoons in the bull's neck. But this time, the Spaniard chose to set the banderillas himself. He placed three sets, two to a set of these wooden dowels with steel harpoon-shaped tips. Running at the bull from an angle, raising his arms over the horns, he snapped the banderillas with a swift motion of his wrists, setting them close together — within a hand's breadth of each other.

It was a fine performance. There were cheers and shouts of olé, but mostly from the Americans. The Mexicans didn't like the Spaniard because he was a Spaniard.

El Gato then advanced on the bull that had taken up his querencia on the shady side of the ring, close to the wall. Every bull soon finds a querencia — a place in the ring that he likes better than any other, a place where he feels at home. The matador walked one slow step at a time, waving the muleta, until he was less than ten feet from the bull. Still the bull did not move. He stood with his head down, his legs spread out, as if he had gone to sleep.

El Gato took two more cautious steps. He came close enough to flick the bull on the nose with his scarlet cape. He shouted, *"Toro, hooiii."* The crowd began to chant, *"Toro, Toro, Toro."* But the bull with the crooked horn didn't move. The crowd grew restless.

The matador flourished the cape again and shouted, *"Vámonos, Toro."* He tried, *"Toro, hooiii,"* and *"Huh, Toro."* But nothing happened, nothing helped.

Angered by the bull who refused to fight and by the hostile crowd, El Gato suddenly arched his back, threw out his chest, lifted one hand in despair, raised his chin in a gesture of disgust. The disgust was meant for those who had bred the bull, the bull itself, and for the sweltering crowd that was unfriendly.

The crowd took up the challenge. There was a rustling at first, which I thought was the wind, but it quickly turned into a chorus of whistles. A cushion sailed into the ring and fell at the matador's side. Then the air was filled with cushions.

Morales was on his feet, shouting through his cupped hands, "Bag of suet! Owl dust!"

The Spanish matador picked up the first cushion, the one that lay beside him, and contemptuously tossed it over his shoulder. He made a flourish with his cape

11

that flicked the bull's nose, then turned his back on the bull and strode away.

The clamor was ended by a bugle call. It came from the Presidente's box, and the Presidente, the man in charge of the bullfight, a happy, round little man in a cutaway coat and a carnation in his buttonhole, held a white hand aloft.

El Gato stood with his montero against his chest, facing the Presidente. Members of his troupe stood on each side of him.

The pronouncement was brief.

"For conduct unbecoming to the *fiesta brava*, El Gato is fined the sum of two thousand pesos," the Presidente said.

The pronouncement pleased everyone, everyone except Lieutenant Morales.

"Two thousand pesos," he sneered. "It should be a ticket to Alaska. A one-way ticket."

There were more catcalls, more cushions, but El Gato paid no attention. He bowed to the Presidente, put his montero back on his head, straightened his pigtail. His sword handler gave him a sword and he walked across the ring, challenged the bull again, then killed it with one neat thrust.

While they were hitching the chain to the bull's horns, Morales said, "You know, Señor, that the matador does not pay the fine? It's in the contract that the promoter pays the fine — all the fines. What a joke! What fakers! There should be laws against such brigands."

Sand and dust were blowing and it was hard to see across the arena. Morales fanned himself with his hat. The hat was gray and wide, the kind that Mexican cattlemen wear. He also wore cattlemen's stitched, high-heeled boots. He wanted to look like a Mexican cattleman, I guess. But he was a good detective. He had pride and a memory for faces. I felt sure that he would turn up something on Ernesto de la Sierra, providing there was anything to turn up.

3

The Mexican flag and all the pennants around the rim of the arena stood straight out in the wind, as if they were made of wood. The matadors poured water on their muletas and dragged them in the dirt to make them heavy. A muleta that fluttered or moved when it wasn't supposed to, or moved in the wrong direction, could bring quick death.

The fifth and last bull of the afternoon — Morales complained because six bulls had been advertised — weighed 1075 pounds.

The bull's name was Tiburón Negro. When two minutes went by and Black Shark didn't come through the gate, the crowd began to chant, *"Tiburón Negro, Tiburón Negro, donde está el toro grande?"*

The gate was across the ring from us, and the tunnel where the bull would enter. The tunnel was very dark and I couldn't see inside it. The man who had opened the gate stood peering into the darkness. He was ready to close the gate as soon as the bull came through.

The chant went on. The two matadors were across the ring from the tunnel. Their backs were against the barrera and the folds of their capes trailed on the ground. El Burrito was alert, but the Spaniard didn't seem to care whether the bull came out of the tunnel or not.

A cloud of red dust swirled across the ring and into the stands. The chanting faded away. It was very hot. Some of the crowd was drifting toward the exits.

Lieutenant Morales said, "The management has sent to Hermosillo for another bull. It should arrive by tomorrow afternoon."

A man in back of us said, "They are raising another bull in Spain and it will be here next year."

Below us, in the narrow passageway that runs around the arena between the first row of seats and the ring, a scuffling started up between two men. Someone shouted. A woman screamed.

A young man, a boy, was jumping over the wall. He landed on his feet and staggered a moment, then struck out across the ring, dragging a red muleta behind him.

He was tall and thin and had an awkward way of running. He toed in with both feet, but he ran fast. Before any of the attendants could gather themselves, he was at the mouth of the tunnel — not more than thirty feet from the gate that the bull would come through. There he went to his knees, facing the tunnel, and began to brandish the scarlet muleta.

15

The crowd fell quiet. In the quiet the boy's words rang clear. *"Huh, Toro. Huh, Toro. Hola! Tiburón Negro!"* the boy shouted.

There is a no more dangerous place in a bullring, nor a moment of time during a bullfight, than at the gate when the bull charges out of the tunnel.

At that moment, before the picadors break down the great muscle in his neck and the banderilleros with their steel-tipped darts injure him more and the matadors exhaust him with their capes, at that moment he is fierce in all of his strength and spirit. He is determined to kill everything within his sight and he is well capable of doing so.

Cries of "No. No. No." came from the crowd.

Attendants scurried out from behind the wooden burladeros. The two matadors advanced across the ring to intercept the bull. They had reached the center of the ring when he burst through the gate.

He was big and black, black as the mouth of the tunnel he came out of. As many bullfights as I have seen, I am still amazed at the speed of a fresh bull. It is awesome.

The boy was on his knees, facing the bull at the mouth of the tunnel. Not sidewise, not in profile, which would have given the bull a smaller target, but facing the bull. Never is this done. Yes, once. I remember reading about it. Dominguín did it in the ring at Seville.

16

But Dominguín was a famous torero, not a boy scrambling out of the crowd.

As the bull burst into the sunlight, the boy held out the muleta. He grasped it in both hands, his left hand across his chest, his right hand held out. The muleta had not been wet down. And it was not much of a muleta — a light piece of scarlet cloth that he must have found somewhere and sewn together himself.

"A *loco*," Morales said. "Most of the time we have one of these *locos* running around in the bullring."

"No. No. No," the crowd shouted. It was like the sound of firecrackers.

The boy knelt there with his chin on his chest and his back arched and his feet together. His left knee was slightly in front of the other.

His hair hung to his shoulders. A gust of wind whipped it across his eyes. Calmly he took one hand from the muleta and brushed it away and pushed a strand behind his ear to hold it there. I have never seen anyone so calm. I was sure that he had posed like this before. He had practiced it over and over, in some alley or backyard, in front of a mirror at home, until he had developed the posture of a great matador. I felt that he would rather kneel there and be gored than run away or ask for help.

And I was right, though it was the first time — there in the bullring at Tijuana — that I ever saw Manuel

Castillo. I remember asking myself, "What could make a boy jump into a ring and challenge a fighting bull? What possibly? How could a boy not more than sixteen kneel there calmly and face death?" Almost a year has passed since that afternoon and many things have happened between Manuel Castillo and me. But I am not sure even now that I know what the answer is.

For all of his composure the boy was in danger. The crowd knew it and he must have known it, too.

Once in perhaps fifty times, an experienced matador might get away with this foolhardy stunt at the gate. Once in a dozen times a matador might confront a fresh bull in the center of the ring, far from the safety of the barrera, using the cloth in a dangerous pass against a bull that was much wiser than when he came into the ring. But to do both and hope to come out alive was asking a lot of providence.

Two minutes may have gone by since the bull lunged through the big red gate. Perhaps it was only half that time. But it was time enough for the matadors to reach the bull and, with cape and muleta, lure him slowly away.

The boy didn't move while the matadors drew the bull off. He knelt with the muleta held in the position he had taken up when he was waiting for the bull, as if he expected the bull to charge again.

A cloud of dust swirled around the boy and he disappeared from sight. When the dust cleared I saw that two attendants had him in tow. He didn't put up a struggle, but strode along stiffly, his chin in the air, looking straight ahead.

4

Morales' white teeth flashed. He was angry. He stared down at the boy who was walking slowly and stiff-legged toward the barrera, at the two attendants trying to hurry him along.

"I have seen the one who drives on the wrong side of the road," Morales said. "I have seen the one who plays roulette with a loaded pistol. But the one who jumps into a bullring and kneels at the gate and waits for the bull to come out, that one, Señor Delaney, in my life I have never seen before. I would like to see him closer. I would like to talk to this one for a while."

Morales stood up, motioning me to follow. We were perched high up near the Presidente's box and, as we made our way down through the crowd, things began to happen.

The two matadors came to life. The spectacle of a boy — he couldn't have been more than sixteen — a boy in tennis shoes and a homemade cape facing a fresh bull must have flicked their pride. They were out in the middle of the arena, taking turns with the bull.

I didn't get more than a glimpse or two of them as I followed Morales down. Going from the top to the bottom of the Tijuana bullring is like descending into the Grand Canyon. But once I saw the horns graze El Burrito's chest, as he did a slow turn with the cape. And when we reached the callejon and I was hurrying along trying to catch up with Morales, I got another glimpse of him.

The crowd had been screaming. Now there was a sudden hush. There wasn't a sound. El Burrito lay in the dust and the bull was standing over him pawing at his face.

Morales ran down the callejon and I followed at his heels.

Already there was a crowd jammed up at the door of the infirmary. The door was open and lights were being turned on. Inside people were moving around getting things ready for the wounded matador when they carried him in. A priest was standing against the wall.

We went past the infirmary and down a dark corridor to a door with a weak light hanging above it. We went into a small room that was bare except for a table and a few chairs and had a sour smell and one dusty window with bars on it. It was a place where they kept drunks until the wagons arrived to take them to the calabozo.

Two drunks were lying on the floor. A policeman was seated at the table with a yellow pad on it. The boy, who had just been brought in, was standing in front of the table held there by the two attendants who had collared him in the arena.

Morales told the attendants to disappear, which they did. He walked around the table and stood behind the policeman where he could face the boy.

"Does he have a name?" Morales asked the policeman.

"I haven't found one yet," the policeman replied.

"What is your name?" Morales said to the boy.

"Manuel Castillo."

I had heard the boy's name before. He belonged to one of the Chicano gangs up in Mar Vista, but I knew nothing about him.

Morales looked at him carefully, from sneakers to long hair. "Are you *loco*?" he asked. He spoke seriously as if he expected a serious answer.

Manuel Castillo brushed the hair out of his eyes and stared back at Morales. He had a long face — a long chin with a cleft in it. But his face was not horselike, not unpleasing — just long and thin. It was his eyes that you noticed the most, however. They were amber, amber and brown, and very large. The whiteness of his skin made them seem even larger.

"Are you *loco*?" Morales asked again.

22

"No," Manuel said.

If I had been in the boy's place, considering every-thing — what had happened and what might happen — I would have been polite and said, "No, sir." But Manuel, from arrogance or ignorance or for whatever reason, said, "No." Just "no."

"Are you drunk?"

The boy held the muleta at his side, trailing on the floor. Morales reached over and snatched it out of his hand and flung it into the corner.

"Are you drunk?" he repeated.

"No."

"Do you realize that you are responsible for the gor-ing?"

"No," the boy said.

"Well, you *are* responsible. You are the one who aroused the bull. By your craziness you put crazy thoughts in his head. You gave the bull confidence. You gave him an education, flapping around out there with the cape. That is why the goring took place."

Manuel didn't seem to follow Morales' reasoning. Nor did I, for that matter.

"Do you understand what I say?"

"No."

Morales gave the boy a slap across the jaw. It must have stung, but Manuel didn't change his expression.

"Do you understand that?"

23

"Yes," the boy said, speaking in English. "I understand."

"What do you understand?"

The boy was silent.

Morales glanced at the policeman and at the two drunks lying on the floor and then at me. He shrugged his shoulders. He wanted us all to bear witness to the fact that he was dealing with a real crazy.

Brushing his hair back from his eyes, the boy glanced at me over Morales' shoulder. I guess he thought I might help him in some way. Because of my glasses, I guess, which have heavy rims and make me look sympathetic.

Morales stared at the boy for a while, shaking his head. Then he reached in his back pocket and took out a pair of bright thin handcuffs and slipped them onto the boy's wrists.

"Have you sent for the wagon?" he asked the policeman.

"It is outside. But it has a flat tire. It is the left front tire that is flat."

"I do not care which tire is flat, left or right, front or back. Fix it!"

Morales nodded to me and took the boy by the arm. We went along the corridor that led to the infirmary. People were still milling around outside the door, waiting for news from the doctors. It was quiet in the dark corridor. Morales knocked at the door softly. When it opened he pushed the boy and me through.

The room was small. It should have been cool, being there in the bowels of the arena below the ground, but it was very hot. There were a lot of people standing around the walls, mostly the picadors and banderilleros from El Burrito's troupe. From the ceiling in the center of the room hung a big lamp with a lot of bulbs. The lamp gave off a blue white light that made all the faces look sickly.

There was an operating table in the center of the room, under the big lamp, and around it were women nurses and some male nurses and a doctor.

I had read somewhere — why do I like to read about bullfighting but don't like to watch it? — that El Burrito carried his own doctor along with him wherever he fought, even when he went to Spain or South America. A good idea, no doubt, because not all places have a doctor. The great Manolete, who was gored fighting in the small town of Linares, would have lived, so I have heard, had there been a doctor handy. As it was, they had to take the famous torero twenty miles over a dirt road while he bled to death.

Morales had the boy tightly by the arm and he pushed him up as close as he could get to the table where El Burrito was laid out. I stood against the wall but I was close enough to see that the young matador had a hole

25

in his thigh. They had cut his tight silk pants away and the leg was bare.

The hole where the bull's horn went in was not much larger than a silver dollar and blue. But the bull had lifted him into the air and shaken him so that the horn ranged around in several directions. The hooking tore away much of his thigh.

There was the smell of some strong disinfectant and a smell that I didn't recognize.

It was very quiet in the room, but every minute or so El Burrito would raise his head a little and look at his doctor and say, "Señor, am I going to die?" The doctor would always answer him, though he had a lot of instruments to handle. I couldn't hear what the doctor said but his voice sounded hopeful.

After a while Morales turned the boy around and gave him a shove toward the door. In the blue white light from the big lamp over the operating table I had a close look at the boy. He was looking straight in front of him, at nothing, his chin thrust out, still defiant.

5

We went back to the room where the policeman sat at the desk and the two drunks were lying on the floor asleep.

"The tire," Lieutenant Morales said to the policeman, "is it fixed?"

"In a minute it will be fixed," the policeman answered. "If it doesn't hold the air good I will send and get a new tire."

"That would be a good idea," Morales said.

"How is El Burrito?" the policeman asked.

"How is the Burrito?" the lieutenant said, repeating the question, looking at Manuel. "*Loco*, how is the Burrito? Did you find him in excellent health? Will he be fighting the bulls next week? You are an expert in the matter of the bulls. *Qué pasa, Loco?*"

The boy shrugged his shoulders, but he really wasn't listening to Morales. He stood looking at the muleta that Morales had taken from him and flung into the

27

corner. His face was pale but there was no sign that he regretted what he had done. I had the feeling that he would do it again if he got the chance.

"How old are you, *Loco?*" Morales asked.

"Sixteen years."

"You look older. You could be twenty. How old are you, *Loco?*"

"Sixteen."

"Where do you live?"

"Across the border. Near Mar Vista. In the U.S.A."

"Where else would he live," Morales said, looking at me. "All the *locos* live in the U.S.A. You have a factory over there that turns *locos* out in great numbers. New models every year."

"Who is your father?" Morales asked the boy.

"He is dead."

"Your mother looks out for you?"

"My stepmother."

"Who else?"

"I have an uncle."

"What does the uncle do?"

"He works in the orchards. Sometimes he picks tomatoes and grapes."

Morales wanted to find out what the boy could raise in the way of a mordida. They all look for bites in Tijuana. The small fish take small bites; the big fish take big bites. Morales was fishing around.

"You have no one else?"

"I have a grandfather."

"What does the old one do?"

"He has a flock of goats."

"You have no brothers or sisters?"

"Two sisters and a half cousin."

"What does this half of a cousin do?"

"He raises chickens and pigeons."

Morales was discouraged. His vision of a mordida had grown dim. "What is the name of this businessman who sells pigeons?"

"Paco Chacon."

"Chacon." Lieutenant Morales said the name slowly. "Paco Chacon. I have heard that before. It rings a bell or two in my head. Does this Chacon drive a pickup? A green pickup?"

"I don't know," Manuel said.

"You have a cousin and you do not know what he drives around in?"

"I don't see him very often."

"When you do see him, what is the color of the pickup?" Morales said.

"White."

"You are colorblind perhaps?" Morales asked.

"Yes," the boy said.

"We have a *loco* who is also blind," Morales announced.

He turned his back on the boy and glanced at me. "This Paco Chacon," he said, "you have encountered him? No? He is about thirty years old and *muy duro*. We got him on marijuana and put him over in the big *calabozo* for six months. He is out now. I saw him last week driving around in the green pickup."

There was something about Manuel Castillo that I liked. But if you had asked me what it was, I couldn't have told you. Not at that moment, certainly, as he stood there in front of the desk half-listening to Morales, answering questions in a listless voice, most of the time with an eye on the muleta that was lying in the corner.

I was aware that the boy would be locked up unless he could buy his way off, which didn't seem likely. There was a good chance that he would be sent to San Tomás prison for a couple of months. But I really didn't mean to get myself into it. I already had a heavy work load — forty-two boys that I was responsible for. All I could take care of. I was really surprised when I heard myself say, "Manuel here lives in Mar Vista. It's my territory. I'll take him home and keep an eye on him."

I expected Morales to object. And I am sure he would have objected if there had been any chance for a mordida, even a small one.

"Take him," he said. "Take him now. I am very tired with these *fritadas medias*. These half-fried potatoes you send us from America."

30

He walked over to the boy and unlocked the handcuffs. He placed a gentle hand on Manuel's shoulder, as a father might do.

"Listen, *Loco*," he said. "Listen to me with care."

The boy looked up hopefully.

"Do you listen?"

"Yes."

"As a great favor to me, do not come back. Tomorrow or next year, do not come back. Or the year after, do not come back. Understand? And tell your half of a cousin, Paco Chacon, to watch his step. When he drives around in his green pickup, tell him to take care."

"Yes," the boy said.

He took one last glance at the muleta and for a moment I was afraid that he was going to ask Morales if he could have it back.

Morales still had a hand on the boy's shoulder. He walked him to the door, opened the door, and shoved him into the corridor.

"*Adiós, Loco,*" he said to the boy. "And remember — do not come back. And do not forget my message to Paco Chacon and his green pickup."

He stepped aside for me to pass and made a slight bow, not deep enough to show his bald spot. "I will look in the files tonight," he said. "And I will say nothing to Simpson if I should see him. *Nada.*"

"I appreciate that, Lieutenant."

31

"But may I impose upon you again to say, confine yourself to the juveniles. They require your help, Señor Delaney. Much help. And stay far away from the dope business. It is a big ache in the head."

Castillo stood with his back to us, a dozen steps away. As I listened to Morales I found myself hoping that the boy would make a break for it. The corridor was dark and filled with people waiting for news about El Burrito. In five seconds he could disappear into the crowd. Five seconds and I wouldn't have another wild Chicano to worry about.

6

The wind had gone down but when I turned on the car lights they rayed out in all directions against a wall of gray dust. And as we went down the main street you could scarcely see the store fronts or the car in front of you.

I drove slowly because I was afraid of bumping somebody or being bumped. If you have an accident in Tijuana you get taken to the calabozo, even if it isn't your fault. That is, you go to jail unless you slip the officer a ten-dollar bill — a twenty is better. The two times I've been in an accident I got off by showing my badge. But if I had an accident now I couldn't very well flash a badge and set a bad example in front of the boy.

We got to the border station without any trouble, but a long line of cars was waiting to go through customs. There was a big drive on against drug smuggling and we had to inch along for almost an hour to get across the border.

The boy said nothing. He sat there with an elbow on the armrest and his chin in his hand, staring out the window. I've never found a Chicano who did very much talking, especially to an officer, so it didn't bother me. The only time we came close to talking was when I offered him a cigaret and he shook his head either that he didn't want one or he didn't smoke, I didn't know which.

Four or five kids came up and hung around the car as we inched along. I know most of them around customs, so they asked me about the bullfights and El Gato and the goring of El Burrito. That may be why the boy didn't say anything.

It was different as soon as we left customs and were in the U.S. Castillo took his elbow off the armrest and gave me a sidelong glance.

"Why did you get me off?" he asked.

I still didn't know why, but I said, "I want to talk to you."

He spoke in Spanish. I speak it well, but I answered him in English. No matter how well you speak the language, there's always an accent. An accent is not a good thing to have if you're speaking to a Chicano for the first time. It gives them a hold over you, a feeling of superiority. Later on, after they get to know you, then it is a good thing to be able to speak Spanish. Then they feel closer to you somehow. They feel a little sorry for

34

you because you have a small accent and they don't have any.

I didn't expect him to thank me for the trouble and he didn't.

"Understand," I said, "you didn't get out of the bullfight business because I have a big heart. I want to talk to you about some things. We can talk about them now or we can talk at the station."

He took his time about answering. I think he was surprised that I wasn't just some big-hearted character with nothing better to do than to go around getting kids out of trouble.

"*Ahora*," he finally said.

"Now."

"Now," he said in English. "And I am very hungry."

It's a funny thing about the bullfights. It's not like baseball or football where half the fun is eating hot dogs and peanuts. At a bullfight, you never get hungry. It must be the blood flying around.

I slowed down and started to pull into the first eating place we came to, but Castillo said that the food there was crummy, that the next place was better. It was called El Sombrero. I went on to the Sombrero and parked. It had a huge neon sign in the shape of a hat on the roof, but you could barely see it through all the dust.

There was a counter along one side of the café and

Castillo headed for it. I wanted a little privacy, so I caught his arm and steered him to a booth on the other side of the room. A girl dressed up in a Mexican outfit came to take our order. I asked for a steak and french fries and salad. Without looking at the menu, Castillo ordered a tuna sandwich and a Coke.

"If you eat like this all the time, no wonder you're skinny," I said.

I was sitting across from him in the booth and the light was good. It was the first chance that I had had to really look at him.

"Do you know Ernesto de la Sierra?" I asked him.

"Yes."

"How well?"

"I see him."

"How often? Every day? Once a week? Once a month?"

"Once a month."

"No more than once a month?"

"I used to see him at school every day. That was before we dropped out."

"You both dropped out?"

"Yes."

"Where do you see him now?"

"Over at the playground once in a while. Other places."

"At the cockfights?"

The Chicanos around San Diego have a regular circuit of cockfights. Usually they meet every Saturday night at one or another of several places along the border. Cockfighting, as you probably know, is illegal in California. As far as I know it's illegal all over the United States, except for a couple of states.

Castillo took his time answering.

"Do you ever see Ernie at the cockfights?" I asked him again.

"Once," Manuel said.

"Has he ever sold you marijuana?"

"I don't smoke it," he said.

"No, but has he ever tried to sell you?"

"I don't remember," he said, suddenly suspicious.

"He has or he hasn't?"

"Don't ask me that. I'm not a fink."

All the time we were talking he kept glancing toward the counter. There were no customers seated at the counter so after a while I figured he must be looking at the girl who was polishing a big chrome coffee maker. My hunch was correct because, when our food came, the girl who had been doing the polishing brought it, not the waitress who took our order.

The girl put the tuna sandwich and the Coke in front of Castillo. As she set them down he asked her if she had been to the bullfights.

"Sure," she said. "I just got back."

"Who did you go with, Yvonne?"

"Marlon Brando, of course. Who do you think?" She spoke in a little girl's voice.

"What happened to Elvis Presley?" Manuel asked her.

"He don't like bullfights," she said and put my steak and salad on the table.

"Who did you go with? Sure enough."

"Gladys," she said. "Does that make you feel better? Gladys and I went together."

She gave the table a quick glance and went off toward the coffee machine.

My steak was small and tough. I had a hard time cutting it.

"Is Yvonne why you jumped in the ring?" I asked Manuel.

"I would have jumped anyway. Whether she was there or not."

He held up one hand as if he were taking an oath.

"Then why did you jump into the bullring?"

"Because I am *loco*. Just like Lieutenant Morales said, I am *loco* in the head."

I was beginning to think that he *was* loco and maybe that was what he wanted me to think. But if he was crazy, I was pretty sure that it was because of the girl. He couldn't keep his eyes off her. He didn't touch his tuna sandwich. He did drink his Coke, gulping at it every now and then, but his eyes were on her all the time.

Either way, I decided that there wasn't much point in me trying to get anything out of him while Yvonne was around. So I forgot about it and ate my dinner.

When Yvonne came back she had another Coke, this one in a bigger glass. "I knew you would be asking for a second," she said, putting the glass down.

"Thanks, Yvonne," he said.

His voice hushed when he thanked her, as if she had done him some momentous favor.

"How many of these you drink a day?" she asked.

"Two or three."

"Two or three, my eye. More like a dozen."

"I'd drink a dozen if you brought them, Yvonne."

As Yvonne reached down to pick up his empty glass, the boy touched her hand.

"No," she said, jerking her hand away. "I don't like that when I'm on duty."

The boy didn't seem to mind her display of anger. I guess that just touching her hand was enough for him.

His lips moved silently for a moment and I realized for the first time that he stuttered. He didn't make any preliminary noises like most stutterers. He just moved his lips until he had all the words in the right place and shape before he said them.

39

"Did you see the fight?" he asked Yvonne, trying to be casual about it.

"Yes," Yvonne said.

"Did you see me kneeling at the gate?"

"Sure."

"How did you know it was me?"

Yvonne laughed as if she thought he was asking a foolish question. She had blond hair that was puffed out in the shape of a beehive. It teetered on her head when she laughed.

"How did you know me?" he repeated.

"How? Who else in the world would get down right in front of the gate where the bull comes out? Down on his knees fifty feet from the tunnel."

"Thirty feet," Manuel corrected her.

Yvonne tightened her lips and shivered a little. "It was awful," she said. "Gladys screamed but I was so scared I couldn't make a sound."

"I was scared, too," Manuel said.

"Only brave men get scared," Yvonne said. "If you are scared and then are brave, it means more than if you are just brave."

Manuel sipped his Coke and seemed to think about this for a while. Then he said, "I would have killed the bull if they hadn't butted in. I was going to dedicate it to you."

"That would have been a big honor," Yvonne said.

"I've never had a bull dedicated to me. When I was in junior high my boy friend was a pitcher and he pitched a no-hitter and dedicated it to me. But I've never had a bull dedicated to me."

"I guess now you never will," Manuel said. "They are going to throw me in jail if I go down there again."

Yvonne smiled. She had pretty teeth, white and regular as kernels of Oregon corn. "I'll pretend that you dedicated the bull to me. You were very brave. It was the biggest thrill of my life. Gladys said you were *mucho macho.*"

Manuel waited for her to go on, but she got busy straightening up the table.

"What did you say?" Manuel asked.

"I said *macho,* too. *Mucho macho.*"

Macho, this was the word he must have been waiting to hear. He finished his Coke in one gulp. His face glowed. He seemed to expand and for a moment I half-expected to see him go floating off in the air.

I was familiar with the word macho, with machismo. I had run into it in some form or other in most of the young Chicanos I'd had anything to do with during my time with the department. It's behind many of the gang wars, the school fights, the knifings and killings that take place along the border.

I am not sure where this machismo business started. Some say that it started a long time ago with the Spanish conquistadores — when Pizarro came to Peru and Hernando Cortez came to Mexico. Others say that it's related to the days of chivalry when knights jousted and killed each other for a lady's favor.

But as I have seen things happen around here on the border, there's a big difference between the two, between chivalry and machismo. The knight courted a lady and fought for her. If he won her, it was the highest happiness. The machista fights for a woman against another man. But in this fight the woman is only an excuse. She is not important. It is the defeat of the rival that's important.

It was possible that Manuel was not just another wild kid looking for excitement. The stunt in the bullring could be pure machismo. It could also be something else.

I sat thinking about it, chewing on my tough steak, while Yvonne brought Manuel another tuna sandwich. She begged him to eat it and he did. I might as well not have been there for all the attention they paid me. By the time I finished my steak I was certain that Manuel had a rival. I wasn't surprised at all when the rival walked into the café. I was only surprised that it was Ernie Sierra.

7

I had paid the bill, leaving a bigger tip than usual, and was standing at the counter. Yvonne asked me how the steak was and I said that they must have taken it off one of the bulls they had killed that afternoon. I was standing there at the counter when I felt a gust of hot air come streaming through the front door.

I couldn't see who walked in, but whoever it was left the door open and a man at the end of the counter yelled, "Shut the door. Where was you raised? In a barn?"

It was a familiar remark. Usually it went unchallenged, but in this case it was said to the wrong person. Before he had taken two steps into the room I recognized Ernie Sierra. He was alone, dressed in his white pullover with an insignia of an owl stitched on it and tight-fitting black stretch pants.

The man at the end of the counter repeated his remark. Ernie turned as if to close the door, then decided not to, and came slowly up the aisle toward the counter.

He had a lot of black hair trimmed long on the sides and down the neck, and a thin mustache that drooped at the ends. He hunched his shoulders a little as he walked, like a boxer. His eyes darted around at the booths that had now filled up, looking for the man who had told him to close the door.

Before he reached the counter, he spotted me. He didn't let on that he saw me, but his expression changed and he stopped swaggering. He walked past without speaking and sat down at the counter.

Yvonne went over and shut the door. When she came back she didn't say anything, as if she was used to shutting doors after Ernie Sierra. The man at the end of the counter, who had yelled at him, didn't say anything, either.

Yvonne handed Ernie a menu and went over to the machine and drew a mug of coffee. When she put the coffee in front of him, he ordered ham and eggs, over easy. He didn't look at her when he spoke, keeping his eyes on the counter. Yvonne went out to the kitchen and I heard her repeat the order. She didn't come back, but I caught a glimpse of her peering through the glass in the kitchen door. I thought it was smart of her to stay in the kitchen.

Ernie took a swallow of his coffee and lit a cigaret. I noticed that he had a diamond ring on his little finger. It struck me as odd that a sixteen-year-old would be wearing a diamond. And a good-sized diamond at that.

Ernie still hadn't let on that he saw me. He took a drag on his cigaret and glanced up through the smoke at Manuel.

"How's the matador?" he said. "You're looking pale."

Manuel was silent. I had a feeling that he didn't want to get into an argument.

"You were lucky this afternoon, my friend."

"Why lucky?" Manuel said.

"You didn't get killed, did you? That's lucky."

"Lucky for me," Manuel said. "But not so lucky for you."

"Lucky for me, too," Ernie said. "You're my favorite matador. You are a great one with the bull. I'll feel very sorry when you get killed. I'll buy you a big bouquet of lilies."

"What will you use for money?" Manuel asked.

Ernie didn't say anything for a moment or two, not until Yvonne brought in his order. Then he reached in his pocket and pulled out a wad of greenbacks, neatly stacked together and held by a gold money clip. He took his time and selected a twenty from the stack and dropped it on the counter to pay for his ham and eggs.

He must have had a thousand dollars in his pocket. The sparkler on his little finger could have cost two thousand. I think it was at this moment, with the big diamond glittering in my eye, that I pretty much gave

45

up on Ernie Sierra. He was on the road to the Joint and there wasn't much that I could do to stop him.

"What did you do," I asked him, "hold up a bank?"

Ernie looked over at me and laughed, a little embarrassed that he hadn't spoken before.

"My aunt up and died," he said. "She was rich and lived in Tepic. She died and left me a pot full of pesos."

"You told me about your aunt one time," I said. "Her name was Olivia Tovar, if I remember."

"That's the one," he said. "I have two other aunts but they're poor."

"Come in tomorrow and we'll talk about the money," I told him. "You should have some advice about what to do with it."

"What time, Mr. Delaney?"

"Ten."

"That's fine; I'll be there. Thanks, Mr. Delaney. I sure need advice."

While he was putting his money away, I nudged Manuel and we started for the door.

"I'll send you a dozen bouquets," Ernie called out to Manuel.

Manuel held up his hand and gave him the finger and we went outside. Manuel closed the door.

Some of the dust had settled but the night was still hot and there was a wind whipping around high up in the palm trees.

"Where do you live?" I asked Manuel.

"Over in Tres Gavilanes."

"That's ten miles."

"More like fifteen. But you don't have to take me home. I'll hitch a ride. Maybe Yvonne will take me. I'll wait around."

I didn't want him to hang around the café and get into a fight with Ernie Sierra. I had no desire to take him home, fifteen miles over country roads. And I didn't want to put him in jail on the strength of the escapade in Tijuana.

I decided to do what I had done with other boys several times before. To take him to my house for the night. It usually works out. I get information I couldn't get any other way. I guess it's the friendly atmosphere that makes the boys feel like talking. Some of them have even thanked me afterward.

There have been a few exceptions, of course. Alfonso Rojas, for instance. We had him for two days in our home and everything was going fine. But when he left he took our portable TV along. My wife, Alice, got the TV by saving blue-chip stamps for more than three years and it made her real mad.

"That's the last delinquent you're going to bring into my house," she said. "Ever."

"We've had about a dozen boys," I replied, "and Rojas is the only one that let us down."

"You're forgetting Harold Jensen," Alice said.

"Harold was never in our home," I said.

"No, thank goodness, but it's the same thing."

It wasn't the same thing, although I guess that it was pretty close to being the same. Anyway, it wasn't good. In fact, it was bad. It was bad enough to cost me my job as detective with the Mar Vista Police Department.

It happened this way. Harold Jensen and I were coming down from San Quentin prison. He was a young man from San Diego and I had known him for a long time, gone to school with him and everything. I was bringing him down to San Diego to testify in a trial. It was July and we were coming through Bakersfield, which is very hot in July. Jensen said he would like to have a beer.

It seemed like a good idea and I pulled into a café where they had a beer sign in the window. Jensen had on handcuffs. If you have ever tried, you know it's pretty hard to drink a beer in a pair of handcuffs. Since I had known him for a long time and gone to school with him, as I have said, I unlocked the cuffs.

Jensen had two beers but I had only one. I was careful to keep my wits about me. After his second beer Jensen said he was going to the toilet and I told him to hurry it up because we were running late and still had a couple of hundred miles to go.

He was gone two minutes. I know because I glanced

48

at my watch. After three minutes had gone I went looking for him. He wasn't in the toilet. There was a small window over the washbowl. It was so small that I could never figure how he wiggled through it. The screen was torn out and when I went outside I found footprints in the dirt where he had jumped down.

The Bakersfield police picked Jensen up inside of a week, but that didn't help me any in Mar Vista. Everyone on the force tried to be sympathetic but I still lost my detective job. That's how I got into parole work.

I wasn't sure just how Alice would take Manuel Castillo. But I sort of liked the boy and was willing to take a chance that she had gotten over being mad about Rojas and the portable TV.

We live in Mar Vista, on the outskirts, and we were there in ten minutes. It was only about eight o'clock and Alice was grading history papers. She is very conscientious about her students and spends a lot of time going over their work. I had phoned her from the café, so she wasn't waiting supper. But I hadn't said anything about Castillo.

When we went into the house, while I was introducing Castillo, I was careful to give Alice the impression that I wasn't planning to keep him longer than overnight.

I needn't have bothered. Alice took to the boy right off. He had a friendly way about him which was really sincere. She even asked him what he had eaten at the café and when he told her she insisted that he eat a piece of apple pie and ice cream.

She took to him so much that I had a hard time getting rid of her. It was all of nine thirty before she left us alone.

8

We sat down in the den and Manuel asked me if he could turn on the radio and listen to some rock. I told him that I didn't want to listen to rock until later, until we got through with our talk. In an offhand way I let him know that I could still take him down to Juvenile Hall and book him.

I started off by saying, "I know about your family from what you told Lieutenant Morales. But I don't know much about you. You've dropped out of school. To do what? To take a job?"

"No."

"Are you looking?"

"I'm looking around."

"What about the bullfighting?"

"I don't know."

"But you want to be a matador. Don't you?"

"It takes a long time."

"Everything takes a long time," I said, thinking of

myself, of the years I had spent on the Mar Vista Police Department with nothing much to show for it. "In some cases it takes a lifetime."

"I don't want to wait that long."

"Maybe you should go to Pamplona."

"Where's Pamplona?"

"It's in Spain. A town where they let the bulls loose in the street and everybody becomes a matador, quickly. You chase the bulls and bulls chase you."

"That doesn't sound like much fun. Chasing bulls around in the street."

"When you jumped in the ring this afternoon," I said, "that must have been to impress Ernie. You have a feud on, don't you?"

"Sort of."

"Ernie is an Owl. What do you belong to?"

"The Conquistadores."

"I've heard of them."

We had pretty well tamed the gangs in Mar Vista. We began taming them when I was a detective and now things were pretty quiet. That is, the gangs weren't out killing each other every other night. This didn't mean that they still weren't around, that you could be a Chicano and get by on your own. If you were poor and lived on the wrong side of the tracks you belonged to a gang. You had to belong if you wanted to keep on breathing.

"Where does Ernie Sierra rate with the Owls?"

"Number One."

"Where are you with the Conquistadores?"

"Number Two," Manuel said, "but maybe I'll be Number One pretty soon."

"When they hear about you fighting the bull?"

"*Es posible.*"

He kept an eye on the radio and after a while I told him to turn it on. He got a rock station in Mexico and turned the volume down low so we could talk. He quit fidgeting around now and began to listen to me for the first time.

I asked him what school he had gone to and learned that it was the Mar Vista High School, which is located just two blocks from where I live.

"Why did you quit? Or did you get kicked out?" I asked him.

"I quit."

"Why?"

"I wasn't learning anything."

"What do you want to learn that you weren't learning?"

Manuel thought for a while. "I was just wasting time," he said. "I don't know what I want to learn."

"Mar Vista High is a good school," I observed. "Speaking as a taxpayer I can say that it should be good.

We spend enough money on it. There must be something there that's worth learning for all the money we taxpayers put out."

"I read about Coronado in my history class," Manuel said. "He was the Spaniard who started out from Mexico 'way back in 1539. He had a big army and they went up and fought the Zuñi Indians where Arizona is now and one of his men found the Grand Canyon. Then they went on as far as Kansas. They were looking for the Seven Cities of Cíbola. I would like to have been with Coronado looking for the Seven Cities."

"He never found them," I said, in defense of education. "And when he came back to Mexico they arrested him for stealing a horse. One horse, mind you. And he had spent almost a million dollars of his own money outfitting an army. They tried him and convicted him and he died when he was only a young man."

"I like Coronado," Manuel said. "If he was here now and wanted someone to go and look for the Seven Cities or look for anything, I would go."

Manuel was excited about Hernando Cortez, too, and the way he conquered Mexico, almost singlehanded. And also Pizarro who conquered the Inca and Peru. And Guzmán who discovered Colombia and cartloads of gold. We talked about all of them, on and on until nearly twelve. When we turned off the radio and said good

54

night, I had the feeling that Manuel Castillo had been born in the wrong century. He should have lived four hundred years ago, in the time of the conquistadores.

I slept soundly. When I went out to the kitchen to make coffee, I found a note on the kitchen sink, scrawled on a paper bag.

"Good-by. Thanks for the supper last night. Thanks for letting me sleep in your house. I liked our talk but a lot of the time I felt like a fish on a fish line.

Your friend,
Manuel Castillo."

Alice came into the kitchen shortly afterward, but I put the note in my pocket and didn't say anything about it. I told her Manuel had to leave early and that he had thanked us for our hospitality.

"He's a nice boy. I like him," she said. "Somehow he reminds me of Mark."

Mark is our son and he's up in Canada now. He's been there for two years. He went there when the draft board called him up for the army. He didn't want to go to Vietnam, so he drove off one morning in his broken-down Ford and kept going until he got to Canada.

"Yes," I said, "when you come to think of it he's a lot like Mark."

"Quiet, for one thing," Alice said. "And serious."

"I'm going over to school and get some more dope on him," I said.

9

Sometime in the night the wind shifted to the west. It was now blowing in from the sea, and the edges of the mountains down in Mexico stood out sharp and clear against a blue sky. After a santana we usually have this kind of a pretty day.

At seven thirty, as soon as they were open, I went over to Mar Vista High School and talked to the principal, Miss Stokes. I talk to her on an average of once a week so we know each other pretty well. She's sixty-four and about ready to retire. I'll be sorry to see her leave.

I told her that I wanted to find out where Manuel Castillo lived. I decided not to say he had spent last night at our house. Miss Stokes has sort of a sad expression usually, but it changed when I mentioned Manuel's name. She even smiled.

"The last address I have for Manny is Los Tres Gavilanes Rojos," Miss Stokes said.

I was interested that a warmth came into her voice that wasn't there before.

"He doesn't have much of a home," she said.

"That's what I understand. I may take a run out that way sometime and see if I can find him."

She gave me a distressed look. "I hope there's nothing wrong."

"Nothing, Miss Stokes."

"I am so glad to hear that. We all love Manny here at the school. I've never been to Gavilanes," she said, "but I have an idea where it is. Won't you come in? I'll draw you a map."

I followed her into her office, which is almost as small as mine, and sat down while she tried to figure out where Gavilanes was.

"It was one of the first Spanish grants in this part of the country," she said. "The original grant from the king of Spain was for forty-seven thousand acres. But there are only about twenty-five acres left and these are worthless. The family has been selling the ranch off piece by piece for a hundred years. At times when it didn't bring more than a dollar an acre. A five-acre piece, which is now right in the heart of downtown Mar Vista, was traded by one of the family for a pair of riding gloves. Imagine, trading land worth millions for a pair of gloves."

Miss Stokes drew me a map of the best way to get to Gavilanes Rojos. The map was neat but vague about distances. As I left she said again that she hoped that Manny wasn't in any trouble. I didn't tell her that I thought he had a good chance of becoming a predelinquent, which is a term we use in the business for someone who, if he keeps on doing what he is doing, will land in jail.

"Maybe you can get him to come back to school," Miss Stokes said.

"I'll try."

After leaving the school I went straight to the station. It was still early and the night sergeant was getting ready to go home. His name is Phelps and he's a portly, good-natured man, easy to work with. Besides this, he was the only one on the force who took my part when I got into the trouble over Harold Jensen.

I asked him if he'd had an easy night.

"The worst I can remember."

"What happened?"

"Chicanos. By the carload."

"Anybody I know?"

He shoved the blotter toward me and I gave it a quick glance — the names, ages, and charges of all concerned. I knew none of them. They all were in their late twenties and therefore no business of mine.

I went into the record office, which is located in an adjoining room, and pulled out the file on Ernie Sierra. There was no entry for him since the first of November, two weeks before. I read the entry over to refresh my mind. Since the new ruling on narcotics, I always felt guilty when I went into the police files. And as luck would have it, just as I was putting the file back, Simpson popped his head in the door.

"You're at it early, Mr. Delaney," he said.

He calls me Mr. Delaney although we have known each other for more than a year — since the day I went into parole work and he got my job as lieutenant.

"I was checking on Sierra's file," I said.

"It's status quo," he said. "But we haven't given up on him yet."

"I'll see Ernie today on my monthly checkup and I wanted to make sure that there was nothing new."

"I put a tail on him last Saturday and they followed him to Tijuana and as far down as Rosarita, but nothing turned up."

Simpson was short and thin and dapper. He spoke quickly and moved around quickly on quiet rubber heels. He smoked a lot, but after he put out a cigaret in the ashtray, he would empty the tray and wipe it clean. He always carried new money. Whenever a bill looked soiled or a coin was tarnished, he would put it away until he could exchange it at the bank for new money. He was very neat and efficient.

"You had him tailed as far as Rosarita," I said. "What was he doing down there, twenty miles below the border?"

"He had some chickens and a crate of pigeons," Simpson said. "He was peddling them to the café there."

"He's not supposed to be in Rosarita," I said. "According to his parole, he's not supposed to travel farther south than Tijuana."

"You'll muck things up for us good if you keep him to that restriction," Simpson said. "Let him wander around where he wants to."

"And violate parole?"

"Sure. Why not? What's more important? Parole or catching a pusher?"

"Parole, if it prevents him from pushing," I said.

Simpson took out four bright silver coins and turned them over slowly in his hand and put them back in his pocket. "My advice to you," he said, "is to forget the parole until we're through with our investigation. If you want an order from the chief to that effect, I'll get one."

I could have said that parole was under the state's jurisdiction and not under the chief of police, but I didn't. I didn't say anything about running into Sierra at the café the night before, either. I closed the file and went down the hall to the desk Chief Barton lets me use part-time.

About ten o'clock I had a call from Sierra. He was working on an emergency job — a school bus that he had to get out before three that afternoon — and would it be all right if he came in tomorrow. I told him that I would drop by the garage and we could talk while he was working on the bus.

Right after that I put in a call for the chief of police in Tepic, which is a good-sized town between Guadalajara and Mazatlán. Usually it takes an hour or so, sometimes a day, to get through to any place in Mexico, but I reached the chief, Señor Gaspar Gonzales, in less than two minutes. At first he had a little trouble understanding me, but I finally got over to him who I was and that I would like a check on a Señorita Olivia Tovar — was she dead or alive? I hung up and in less than an hour the chief called back to say that Olivia Tovar had died on September 20, two months before.

Somehow I was surprised that Ernie Sierra had told me the truth about his aunt's death. I never thought that Ernie was a liar, but still I was surprised.

10

Sierra lived with his uncle in an old ramshackle house on the outskirts of town. Behind the house his uncle had a garage and Sierra worked for him. Chicanos are good mechanics. Whenever I had any work to do, I'd take my car around to the Sierras.

The school bus was parked in the backyard with pieces of the rear end scattered all over the ground. Sierra was underneath. He crawled out and wiped off his hands.

"I'm sorry I couldn't make it," he said, "but everyone wants their car fixed right now. The school's worst of all."

"I know how it is," I said, being friendly. People at the office think I'm too friendly with the boys I have. But I think it pays off.

"I got a little over six thousand from my aunt in Tepic," Ernie Sierra said.

"How much of it's left?"

"Oh, about three thousand eight hundred."

"Do you want to put it in the bank?"

"Sure. I might get some interest on it in the bank."

"There are four of them here in town. They're all good. Pick out one, deposit your money in a time account, and send me a copy of your deposit slip."

"I'll do that tomorrow," Ernie said. "First thing in the morning. And I'll send you the slip."

"Good," I said and started to leave. Then I remembered my conversation with George Simpson. "By the way, I hear that you were at Rosarita last week. You're not supposed to be down there, you know."

"Yes, I know it. But I was in Tijuana with a truck full of chickens and pigeons I couldn't sell and I heard of this café in Rosarita and went down there and sold them."

"It might be a good idea to check with me before you go down again," I said. "I'd like to keep your report clean."

"I only have another fifty-nine days to go on my parole," Ernie said.

"That's right," I said. "So it might be a good idea to watch it."

He walked out to the street with me. On the way he showed me his pen of Plymouth Rocks and a shed with a lot of pigeons sitting around on perches.

"I've made more than four hundred on them in the last three months," Ernie said.

"If you go down to Rosarita," I said, "don't forget to let me know."

"I guess somebody must be watching me."

"It's possible."

I went back to the office, picked up some records, and spent the rest of the afternoon on the phone checking up on four of the forty-two boys I had in my case load. Just before I left the office I had a call from Lieutenant Morales. He had gone over his files and found nothing on Ernesto de la Sierra, but he would keep an eye out and let me know if something turned up.

I didn't believe Sierra's story about his trip to Mexico. Selling chickens and pigeons in Rosarita, because he couldn't find a market for them in Tijuana, was plausible enough. But why, in the first place, did he take them to Mexico to sell? The Mexicans raised chickens and pigeons much cheaper than he could raise them in the United States. And therefore they could sell them cheaper. It might be that his chickens and pigeons were special in some way. The Plymouth Rocks were plump and the pigeons were sleek and had bands on their legs. I am no expert, but they didn't look special to me.

When I got home Alice was already there. Before I could hang up my coat she informed me that Manuel Castillo had let us down.

She has a jar shaped like a castle and made of porcelain that she calls Fort Knox. She keeps it on the

65

windowsill in the kitchen. We drop all our change into it — pennies, nickels, and dimes — and save them for our three-year-old niece to use when she goes to college.

"I know how much was there," she said. "I know because I counted it yesterday. There was exactly three dollars and seventy cents. I counted it again just now and there's only two dollars left."

I hung up my coat and closed the closet door. "That was the custom in the old days," I said.

"What custom? Stealing money?"

"No. The Spaniards always had a jug or a basket somewhere in the house. They kept it full of coins, even gold coins. It was kept for their guests. If someone was traveling through, stopped at the house, and needed a little money, he just dipped in and took what he wanted. It was the custom of the times."

"We're not Spaniards," Alice said.

Probably, the way he was brought up, Manuel Castillo had never heard of this custom of his ancestors. He was broke, most likely, and took what he needed. But I didn't want Alice to think so.

"These are not Spanish times," Alice went on.

"Worse luck," I thought of saying, but I didn't. I just took out a dollar and seventy cents from my pocket, plus two dimes and a nickel I had accumulated that day. I put them in the jug and that ended the argument.

11

The rest of the week when I wasn't thinking about Ernie, I thought about Manuel Castillo. On Monday I took Miss Stokes's map and set out to find him.

Along this part of the Mexican border there are many settlements which are too small to be called villages. The Spanish word barrio describes them better. Barrio in Spanish means "a district" or "quarter" or "suburb." Anyway, there are a lot of these shacky settlements. They extend eastward along the border like a string of blisters.

I followed Miss Stokes's instructions until I came to the vague part of her map. Here she had drawn a couple of doodles and beside them had printed the single word "Ask."

I was about two miles off the main highway and headed, according to the position of the sun and the gray crest of the San Pedro de Martír mountains, due south. I was crossing a dry watercourse toward a line of

67

low, fuzzy looking hills. There was not a dwelling in sight. It occurred to me about this time that I was lost.

I climbed out of the watercourse to a shallow rise. At this moment I sighted a man tending a herd of goats. He wasn't far away but between us was a heavy growth of cactus, so instead of getting out of the car I beckoned him over.

He was a toothless old man and he had on a wide straw hat that hid most of his face.

"Los Gavilanes is straight ahead?" I asked him in Spanish.

The old man nodded and beckoned me on with his stick, southward toward the row of distant hills.

Glancing at the empty spaces he was pointing to, I had a second thought. Along the border it is never wise to ask directions in this way. The people are polite, as a rule. If you suggest that a place is in a certain direction, as thoughtlessly I had just done, then they will send you off in that direction rather than take the chance of making an argument of it.

I changed the question and tried again. "Do you know the Castillos?" I asked. "The family lives at Rancho de los Tres Gavilanes Rojos. At the Ranch of the Three Red Hawks."

He had soft, amber-colored eyes and a wandering gaze, which was now fixed upon me.

"The Castillos?" he said, hissing the letters. "There are numerous Castillos, both dead and alive. Which is the one you prefer?"

The old man was looking at the car now, searching for a mark or an insignia — anything that would give him a clue as to who I was.

"Manuel Castillo is the one I prefer," I said.

The old man focused his eyes on me. "Do you come from the school?" he asked.

"No."

"From the police, possibly?"

"I want to talk to him about a matter," I said evading his question. "I talked with Manuel a few days ago, but I would like to talk again."

"Is it a serious talk?"

"You might call it an earnest talk."

"*Serio?*"

"*Sí, serio.*"

A big black goat that smelled bad and had a bell around its neck sidled up and began to nibble on the chrome strip along the side of the car. The old man gave it a clout between the ears and it backed off a step or two and joined the other goats that were bunched up staring at me.

"Los Tres Gavilanes Rojos is behind you, Señor," the old man said. "Return to the road and then turn in the direction of your right hand. Then choose the first turning on your left hand. On that road you will go there. May you go with God."

I thanked the old man and went back to the main road and made the turns. But I still wasn't sure that he had given me the right way. Sometimes the natives give you the wrong way on purpose. Especially if you are an Anglo. Always if they think that you are connected with the law. Anglos and the law are about the same thing to these people. The fact that I was driving an unmarked car helped, but still you have to keep your wits about you in border country. Things are seldom what they seem to be. I daresay that they are never what they seem to be. The old man with the amber-colored eyes, for instance, I met later. He was the grandfather of Manuel Castillo.

After I left the old man, I stopped to ask for directions, still not sure where I was. The place I pulled into was a combination grocery store and gas station with a single pump painted yellow and green outside the door and a couple of old tires lying on the ground.

Inside it was dark. A counter ran along the back and someone was standing quietly behind it, watching me as I walked in. At first, coming in out of the bright sun, I couldn't make out what the person looked like. But after I had picked out a package of gum and a candy bar I saw that it was a young woman with long black hair combed straight down her back.

"I am looking for a place called Los Tres Gavilanes Rojos," I said, speaking in Spanish.

"Los Gavilanes is not a place," she said. "It is a ranch."

Instead of answering me in Spanish she answered in English. This and the tone of her voice put me off, for some reason.

"Whatever it is," I said, "would you tell me where it is?"

Now that my eyes had grown used to the dark, I could see that I was not talking to a woman but to a girl about fifteen.

"Los Tres Gavilanes Rojos is not a place," the girl said again. "It is a ranch and you are on the ranch."

"Good," I said. "Then you can tell me where I can find Manuel Castillo."

"He is not at home," the girl said.

There were calico curtains behind her and a breeze billowed them out, showing a small room and an open door. A moment or two later, when the curtains had settled back, I heard a sound beyond the curtains. Then the closing of a door and then the hoofs of a horse moving away at a quick trot.

"You should come back next week," the girl said. "You waste your time looking for Manuel today."

I paid her money for the candy and gum and she put it into a cigar box. When she looked up I saw that her eyes were the same amber color as the eyes of the old man with the goats, only they were much larger and more luminous. The same as Manuel Castillo's eyes.

"You are a sister of Manuel?" I said.

She put the cigar box away under the counter.

"What is your name?" I asked.

"Conchita."

"Conchita Castillo," I said.

She went about straightening up some cartons that were lying on the counter. She made no effort to correct me so I guessed that I must be right — she was Manuel's sister. Turning her back, she fumbled around with something on the wall and said nothing.

"I need gas," I said, although I had half a tank.

She followed me out of the store and took off the cap. The gasoline had a murky look but nothing big was floating around in it so I said that I would take five gallons. She put the nozzle in the filler and began to pump the handle, one of the slow kind, up and down. I could tell that she didn't like what she was doing.

"This is hard work," I said. "Too hard for a girl. Your brother should be doing this kind of work."

"When he is away, I do it. When he comes back, then he does it and I do nothing."

She was a pretty girl — I guess you might even call her beautiful. She had high cheek bones and a small mouth, but it was her eyes that you noticed most. They were amber-colored and, in the sun, flecked with bright gold.

"Well," I said, hoping to pry something out of her, "your mother must be here."

The girl was cleaning the windshield which was half an inch thick with bugs and red dust. She suddenly stopped.

"Who are you?" she said. "A cop?"

"I'm Ben Delaney from Probation."

She threw away the paper towel she had used on the windshield, which was harder to see through now than when she had started, and glanced at the meter on the one-cylinder pump.

"Two dollars and ten cents," she said, not looking at me.

I gave her three dollars and she went into the store. Another girl came back with my change, a younger girl, but with the same amber-colored eyes, who must have been her sister. I waited around for a moment or two thinking that the first girl would come back. But she didn't so I drove on down the road. There were high weeds on both sides of the road that were covered thick with red dust.

12

At the end of the road there was a big wooden gate with a broken padlock dangling from one of the posts. A pack of lean dogs got up from the shade of a fig tree that had wide-spreading branches and looked to be all of a hundred years old. The dogs stalked over to the gate and peered out at me.

There was a brass bell on the gate. I gave it a tug and waited. After a while a woman in a pink dress appeared from somewhere. She was very fat but moved quickly. She seemed to roll toward me like a pink wave. Without asking me who I was or what I wanted, she opened the gate and invited me in with a flip of her hand.

She led the way and I followed along in her wake to a bench under the mammoth fig tree. I told her that I was a friend of Manuel's and that I had come to talk to him. Manuel didn't look like her but I assumed that she was his stepmother.

"About school?" she said, speaking in Spanish. "He is sixteen and does not have to go to school."

"I have nothing to do with the school, Señora. *Nada*."

She seemed relieved at this. The dogs were circling a few feet away, barking and baring their teeth. Picking up a beer can that lay beside the bench, she flung it at them, along with a ladylike curse. Then she gave me a soft glance and said that she was Manuel's mother.

"He is very nice," she added. "He is really an angel. *Verdad?*"

"Bright," I said, hoping that this would satisfy her.

"He is a boy with much going on up here," she said, tapping her temple.

"*Mucho*," I said.

"*Muchisimo*," she said, getting to her feet. "I will see if I can find Manuel. He is very active, but I will find him for you. Just sit and enjoy the shade."

She went off toward the house leaving behind her a trail of strong perfume.

I sat under the ancient fig tree looking around. What I saw made me feel uncomfortable. Sad and uncomfortable. There were a few acres of weeds that ended in a dry watercourse, a run-down corral, a house with a sagging roof. Beyond the house were crumbling adobe walls and piles of rubble where a larger house once had stood. This was all that was left of Los Tres Gavilanes

Rojos and its 47,000 acres! It made me feel very uncomfortable.

After a while I got up and walked over to the corral where a dozen or so horses were nibbling at a bale of rusty hay. One of the horses was in a lather, having been ridden not long before. A flock of white chickens was walking around under the horses' hoofs, pecking at the straw. Among them were six or seven red roosters. Judging from their clipped combs, their glossy feathers, and strutting walk, I took them to be fighting cocks.

I heard footsteps behind me and turned around. It was Manuel trotting toward me, waving his arms.

"Hola!" he shouted. "You like my roosters?" He came up to the corral out of breath and smiling. "You won't turn me in to the cops?"

"It's not against the law to own gamecocks," I said.

"I know," Manuel said. "But I don't really own these cocks. They belong to the gang and I take care of them."

In the last three months or so the various Mar Vista gangs had taken up cockfighting. Instead of fighting each other, they held cockfights every couple of weeks and let the birds settle their arguments. I doubted if it would last, but for the time being at least it worked and things around Mar Vista were quiet.

"You know about the fights?" Manuel asked me.

"Sure," I said and to make sure he believed me I gave him the particulars. "It was on Admission Day. There were five gangs in it — the Conquistadores, the Owls, Barracudas, Hornets, and Roadrunners. And you had the fights in a barn over at San Benito."

Manuel was a little awed by this information but he tried not to show it.

"Who else knows about the fights?" Manuel said.

"No one."

"You're not going to blab on us?"

"I'll wait and see how it works out. But the first time I hear of a rumble, that's the end of the cockfights."

He jumped into the corral, scrambled around and finally caught one of the roosters. "This is Cortez," he said, holding the gamecock up in front of me. "He's the best we have. We sent away to Alabama and bought him. They shipped him out here by truck."

Cortez was a beautiful bird. His feathers were several shades of yellow and red and they had a hard glossy look as if he were made of metal. Thoughtlessly I put out my hand to touch him. With a movement too quick for the eye, he dealt me a painful blow with his beak.

"Next time when we have a fight," Manuel said, "we're going to use Cortez."

"He'll win," I said, taking a glance at my finger that

was already getting black and blue. Then I brought up what I had come here to talk to him about. "What about school, Manuel? How about going back and giving it another try?"

The question must have surprised him for he put the rooster down and climbed back over the corral and stood looking down at his feet, saying nothing.

"You're an important man in the Conquistadores," I said.

"Number One now," he broke in. "I got elected yesterday at our meeting."

"All the more reason to go back to school. You're a leader. You're big now. How does it look for the big man in one of the two big gangs to be a dropout when all the rest of your gang go to school?"

"How do you know?" he said edgily.

"I looked it up. I went over to school and looked at the list in Miss Stokes's office."

"Where did you get our membership?"

"I know all your gang. First names and last. Ages and residence."

This seemed to impress him, but he still thought I was lying.

"What are the names?" he challenged me.

I have a good memory and I gave him the names, starting alphabetically. "Pepe Alvarado, Jaime Benítez,

78

Chuchu Carrasco, Juan Iturbe, Pedie Palomares, Juan Palomino, Pedro Palou, Jesús Sanchez, and Lalo Ximenez."

Manuel laughed. "You forgot one."

"Who?"

"Jaime Lugo," he said. "We took him in last night."

Manuel kept on laughing over his little joke.

"Did it ever occur to you," I said, "that you're a descendant of a lot of important people? I don't know what your great-great-grandfather did in Spain. But it must have been important."

"He was a general in the army of the king," Manuel said.

"Well, he must have been a good general in the army or the king wouldn't have given him a grant of forty-seven thousand acres."

"And a pension in gold."

"And a pension," I said. "I should think you'd be proud of him."

"I am."

"You don't show it much," I said. "Dropping out of school and all."

Manuel was glancing down at his feet and I didn't pursue the subject any further. It doesn't pay to get on a soapbox with the Chicanos. Give them an idea, something to chew on, but don't rub it in.

Manuel's mother came out where we were standing by the corral but I didn't say anything about school to her, either. She had put some more powder on her face and looked very pretty in her pink dress, though she was certainly fat.

She put an arm around Manuel's shoulder, pulled him to her, and gave him a kiss on the cheek, which he tried to resist.

As I was getting in my car, he asked me to wait a moment. He disappeared into the house and came back in a few minutes with a letter addressed to Yvonne Coleman.

"We don't have a mailman out here," he said. "Maybe you'll mail this for me when you get to town."

Then he reached in his pocket and took out two one-dollar bills and handed them to me.

"I didn't have any money the other morning," he said, "and I had to get something to eat and get as far as Benito on the bus. So I took this out of the bank."

I tried to give the money back but he wouldn't take it.

"The bank's for travelers," I said. "Maybe sometime I'll be traveling out here and need to dip into yours."

"We don't have any bank," he said. "We used to but we don't anymore."

I put the money in my pocket. I couldn't very well tell him that he had only taken a dollar and seventy cents.

13

On my way home I stopped at El Sombrero Café. Yvonne was behind the counter in a new wig that was prettier than the one before. It was jet black and looked like spun glass. It made her face look a little hard but still it was becoming.

She didn't recognize me at first, but when I sat down at the counter and ordered a cup of coffee she blinked her eyes in a friendly way.

"I have a letter for you," I said, tossing it on the counter.

She looked at it suspiciously, swiveling her head, trying to read the handwriting on the envelope upside down. Finally she picked the letter up and tucked it away and brought my coffee.

"I didn't know you were a mailman," she said, giving me a smile that was as thin as a thin knife blade.

"Only on Mondays," I said. "I was talking to Manuel

this afternoon and he asked me to mail it. I brought it instead and saved eight cents."

"Where did you see Manny?"

"At the ranch."

She gave the counter a slow swipe with a towel. "Ernie tells me things are pretty run-down. The ranch, I mean."

I nodded.

"To hear Manny talk it's a regular movie ranch," Yvonne said.

"He's thinking of the days when Los Tres Gavilanes Rojos was a kingdom."

"Ernie tells me it's a weed patch now. A lot of fallen-down walls and weeds."

"That pretty well describes the place," I said.

There was no doubt in my mind that Yvonne was stringing Manuel along, playing him against Ernie Sierra. If it lay in my power I was going to put an end to it. And as I saw the problem my first step was to impress upon her that Manuel was not the heir to a big Spanish ranch. He had probably bragged to her about the ranch, how it was given to his great-great-grandfather by the king of Spain. Forty-seven thousand acres. Hills and streams. Mountains and valleys. And so forth.

"A hundred years ago it took up a good part of the county," I said. "But the family sold it off down through the years." I told her the story Miss Stokes had told me about the five acres that were traded for a pair of gloves. "They gave it away piece by piece," I said.

Yvonne tightened her lips. "They must have been crazy. A real crazy bunch. Manny is a little crazy, too. But he's a good kid."

"Yes," I said. "You've got to remember that he's barely sixteen. His sixteenth birthday was last week."

I was pretty sure that Manuel had told her that he was older than sixteen — eighteen, anyway. And I think I was right because suddenly she got a funny look in her eyes and went off to the kitchen.

When I got home I told Alice about my trip out to Los Tres Gavilanes Rojos and also about talking to Yvonne at the café.

"She's not good for Manuel," I said. "For one thing she's at least three years older than he is. And when you take into consideration that girls are older than boys their same age, it makes a big difference — as much as five years. That's quite a spread."

"I wouldn't get into it if I were you," Alice said. "You can't run his whole life. That part especially."

"But that's the most important part," I said. "Right now anyway. What chance is there of getting him back into school if his mind is mostly stuffed up with a girl five years older than he is?"

We were in the kitchen and Alice was at the stove cooking an omelet with chopped chives and mushrooms and shrimp, little shrimp about the size of your finger-nail, which she does sometimes when we both get home late.

"How do you know that Manuel should be back in school?" she said.

I had to leave college in my junior year, so I never had a chance to graduate. For that reason, maybe, I have an exaggerated idea of what education can do. But I don't think so.

"He had good grades before he dropped out. I saw them. Miss Stokes, the principal, showed them to me. Nothing spectacular, but Manuel's no dummy."

"That still doesn't prove that he should be in school. I have a dozen boys with good grades who should be busy working at something."

"Manuel's busy, all right. But doing what?"

Alice doesn't listen very closely when she is cooking an omelet.

"Doing what?" I repeated. "He's raising fighting cocks and trying to act like a matador."

"In the old days," Alice said, "in the sixteen hundreds and long before that, children were adults by the age of nine or ten. They took their places alongside their fathers and mothers. They worked at the looms and in the fields. If their parents carried stones to build a road or a bridge or a cathedral, they carried stones too."

"We don't carry stones anymore," I said. "We build

bridges and roads out of concrete. And we've quit building cathedrals."

"The family was a working unit," Alice went on. "The young people had their special pastimes and pleasures, but in many other ways they were adults."

"What do you want us to do," I asked, "go back to the Middle Ages?"

"No, but we might borrow an idea or two from them," Alice said. "For one thing, we could quit treating children exclusively as children and give them a few adult responsibilities."

I put the plates and silverware on the table and let that part of the argument drop.

"What bothers me is the girl," I said. "Whether Manuel goes back to school or not, this Yvonne thing bothers me."

"It doesn't sound ideal," Alice admitted.

"She has two boy friends — two that I know about — Manuel and a Chicano named Ernie Sierra. Manuel belongs to the Conquistadores; he's their Number One. And Sierra is Number One with the Owls. Things are quiet. We haven't had a rumble for five months. Everything's nice and peaceful, but this Yvonne business could rip the lid off."

Alice slid a spatula under the omelet and lifted it onto a warm platter. She set it down gently and took

86

off her blue apron and hung it on the back of the door. Alice has pale skin but when she has been working over the stove she gets a lot of color in her cheeks. She looked very pretty. I held the chair out and she sat down and I sat down myself. I usually say a few words of grace but I was so upset over the Yvonne thing that I forgot all about it.

"It seems to me," Alice said, "you're getting yourself in pretty deep with Manuel Castillo. He's not even one of your boys."

"He needs a little direction," I said. "He's not getting much at home."

"But you can't play God with him," Alice said. "It might be good to remember that the great Julius Caesar had a man who did nothing except stand behind his chariot. The man stood there to remind Caesar now and then that he had a bald spot."

Alice is always quoting history at me. I guess it's a natural thing to do, being a history teacher.

I got back at her by taking the two one-dollar bills out of my pocket. I laid them on the table, taking my time, and let her know that Manuel had given them to me.

"Tell me the truth," Alice said, changing the subject. "Does Manuel Castillo really remind you of Mark?"

"Yes."

"Is that why you're trying to help Manuel?"

It was a warm night and we had the windows open. The band was practicing over at the high school. The sounds drifted into the room, and it reminded me of the nights when Mark used to practice for the football games. He played the French horn. I tried to get him to play the sax, but he liked the horn for some reason that I could never figure out.

"Listen, Ben," Alice said, "tell me the truth."

"Yes," I said, "that must be the reason."

"It's funny. Manuel is a Chicano and Mark is an Anglo. And yet they're alike."

"In a lot of ways," I said.

14

One morning about two weeks later Miss Stokes called and asked me if I could come by her office — there was something she wanted to talk to me about. She said she could talk to me over the phone but she would rather see me at the school.

Although it was still November, workmen were already hanging up silver tinsel and red streamers and colored Christmas bells along the main street in Mar Vista. They were starting to decorate the halls at the high school, too, with pine boughs and pine cones covered with fake snow. It was a hot day, too hot to be thinking about Christmas.

Miss Stokes led me into her office and closed the door. From the mysterious way she was acting, I was prepared for something big. Maybe a rumble between Anglos and Chicanos like the one we had last year about this time. The rumble hadn't come off yet or we would have known about it at the office, but trouble could be hatching. It usually took weeks for one of these gang fights to build up.

"You know," Miss Stokes said, "the merchants of Mar Vista have a parade every year, about the first week in December. The schools take part in it, the bands especially. But this year the merchants want to have the Chicano gangs in the parade. What do you think?"

"It might break up the parade," I said. "Break up the town, too."

"That's what I fear," Miss Stokes said.

"But it could do a lot of good. Make better feelings between the gangs. And between the gangs and the town."

"Do you think so? Is it worth a chance?"

"Sure. Let's try," I said. "We only need to get the Owls and the Conquistadores interested. The other gangs will follow along. I'll talk to Manuel and Ernie Sierra."

"Manuel's back in school," Miss Stokes said. "Did you know that?"

"No," I said. "That's good news. You might have him come in after his class and I'll have a talk with him."

I waited for Manuel until the class was over. When he came in and saw me standing there with a smile on my face he looked embarrassed. I wanted to shake his hand and tell him how glad I was that he had returned to school. But I didn't. It wouldn't have worked. So I started right in, as if we had never talked about school, and explained the idea of the parade as Miss Stokes had explained it to me.

"I haven't said anything to any of the other leaders. I wanted to check with you."

Manuel seemed pleased that I had come to him first. "I'll take it up with the members," he said. "We meet on Saturday. But I'll call a special meeting tonight."

"The car dealers will furnish cars for you," Miss Stokes said.

"We'll ride horses," Manuel said.

"The horses would add a lot of color to the parade," Miss Stokes said.

The Conquistadores, in keeping with their name, rode horses wherever they went as a gang. Day or night, on business or pleasure, they went on horseback. It was their mark, the special thing that set them apart from the other gangs around Mar Vista.

The bell rang for the next class and Manuel started for the door.

"You don't have to go to class this moment," Miss Stokes said. "I'll write an excuse for you."

"I'd better go," Manuel said. "My next class is Mr. Hall and geometry. Neither of them likes me very much."

I followed Manuel into the hall.

"How are you making out?" I asked him.

"Not too good."

"It'll be hard for a while," I said. "You've been out of school for half a year. You've gotten rusty. But hang in there . . ."

I was beginning to sound like a football coach before the big game, so I broke off, shook hands with him, and went on my way.

I drove down to Sierra's garage and parked on the street. The uncle was working with a blowtorch, doing something in the back seat of an old Chevy sedan. He quit as soon as I appeared.

"Ernie's not here," he said, looking at his wrist watch which he wore over the cuff of his shirt. "He should be back here later. Sometime this afternoon, maybe."

The uncle's face was shaped like a melon, pitted with small pox scars. He had a hangdog look about him and he mumbled his words as if it were an effort for him to talk. But he had a very sharp, suspicious gaze.

"Nothing important," I said. "I may drop in later. Maybe tomorrow."

"Anything you want to say to Ernie?" the uncle asked me.

"*Nada. No importa.*"

"Very good, Señor. Always glad to see you."

He went back into the garage and I heard the torch pop when he turned it on. He didn't go to work right away. He was still standing there when I drove off. I

92

wondered if he was welding a false bottom on the Chevy. False bottoms were convenient if you wanted to take something illegal across the border and not get caught.

Instead of returning to the office, I drove down to the harbor and parked. I sat there and watched the fishing boats for an hour. Then on a hunch I wrote a note to Ernie, explaining about the parade and asking him to call me when he had a chance. Then I went back to the garage, driving quietly, and parked. The uncle was up in the back seat of the Chevy, bending over his work. He didn't hear me or see me, but somehow he knew I was there. He looked up suddenly, his face shining blue in the light of the hissing torch.

I held up the note I had written. He snuffed the torch out.

"Would you mind giving this to Ernie?" I said, handing him the note.

"I thought it was not important. About Ernie," he said. "Now it is important."

"It is now important," I said. "And by the way, is that a false bottom you're fixing on the Chevy?"

The uncle, whose first name was Carlos, looked surprised. "No Señor. It is an order from a customer. I think he is going to carry gasoline in it. He is going far down in Baja and he requires a place for much gasoline."

"I don't want Ernie to have anything to do with the

work," I said. "It's your business. Not his. Understand?"

"*Sí, sí.* Oh yes, Señor. It is understood that Ernie has nothing to do with it."

"*Nada.*"

"*Nada, Señor . . .*"

A big flock of pigeons — there must have been thirty — swooped low over the yard. The sound of their wings drowned out what the uncle was saying. The pigeons made a turn over the chicken pen, banked, and then were lost against the blue sky.

The uncle followed them with his eyes until they were out of sight. "They will be back," he said. "They always come back."

He walked over to the gate to the pigeon coop and started to unlock it.

Besides raising squabs for sale, I knew that Ernie raised homing pigeons and that he sometimes raced them in meets along the border. As it turned out, the gate to the pen was locked and the uncle had trouble with it.

"Ernie forgot," he said. "Ernie took the key to the lock."

He went away and returned with a handful of keys and tried each one in the lock. In the meantime, the pigeons had wheeled back and were circling overhead, waiting for the gate to open. None of the keys fit the lock.

"Why don't you pry the lock?" I said.

94

"To do that, Señor, will injure it."

"How about the pigeons?"

"They will fly around some more and then they will come back. When they grow tired they will light on the barn and wait."

As he was saying this Ernie drove in. Ernie jumped out of the truck and ran over to where we were standing beside the pen. He looked at his uncle as if he would like to stick a knife in his ribs.

"What goes on? *Qué pasa?*" he shouted.

"You went off with the key," the uncle explained.

"The hell I did," Ernie said. "I gave the key to you and you put it in your pocket."

Castillo felt through his pockets, one after the other, turned them inside out.

"*Nada*," he announced.

"One of these days, old man," Ernie said, "you are going to forget your head. And you know where you are going to find it?"

For some reason the uncle said, "No. Where will I find it?"

"On the ground, uncle. Lying right on the ground. Right under your feet."

I had seen Ernie mad before, but never so mad as he was now. For a minute or more he just stood there speechless, with his hands clasped tight at his sides just staring at his uncle. Then he ran into the shop, came

95

back with a crowbar, and pried the lock off the gate.

"Let's get back and give them a chance to come in," he said. "I let them loose at Del Mar. That's fifty miles, anyway. They're young homers. This is the longest flight they've had."

We stood back from the pen and the pigeons, after a couple of passes, dropped out of the sky one by one. When they were all in the pen Ernie tied the gate shut with a piece of wire.

The uncle went back to work on his false-bottom gasoline tank and Ernie walked out with me to the car. I told him about the parade and that Manuel and the Conquistadores were going to take part in it.

"We march?" he asked me.

"No, you ride. The auto dealers are furnishing the cars."

"What kind?"

"I don't know, but good ones."

"This year's models?"

"The latest," I said. "In all colors."

"Sure. We'll go along with it," Ernie said.

He smiled, but he was still mad over the pigeons. I wondered, as I drove away, why he had to lock them up.

15

Plans for the parade moved along. After I arranged for the Owls and the Conquistadores to take part there was no trouble with the other gangs. The Barracudas, the Roadrunners, and the Hornets would have fought to get into the parade.

And the car dealers came through with the new models — a white Mark IV, a gold Eldorado, a green Gran Prix, a blue Matador, two red Rancheros, a black LTD, a cream-colored Duster, a two-toned Century Regal, three white Capris, three tomato-colored Furies, two red VW buses, and two yellow Volkswagens.

I made the leaders of the gangs draw lots for the automobiles. This eliminated a lot of bickering. At first the plan was for the members to invite their sisters and their girls. But there were far too many sisters, as it turned out, so we restricted the invitations to girl friends.

There weren't many neutral places in the town, places where the gangs could mingle without getting into a fight. Actually, there were only four such places — the Seagull drive-in, Ed's Greasy Spoon, the high school playground, and Shady Lawn Cemetery. I made the gangs agree that the line of march on Main Street and the streets and alleys back to their barrios were neutral ground for the afternoon of the parade. This took a lot of talking and was my one triumph.

Two days before the parade Chief Barton asked me how much protection we were going to need.

"None," I told him.

Chief Barton was a firm believer in force. His idea of protection was to have a policeman behind every telephone pole.

"We had a lot of broken heads last year during the holidays," he said.

"The boys have cooled off since then," I said. "Last year they wouldn't have gone near a parade. I wouldn't even have mentioned it."

"They've cooled off, all right. Something's happened. Whatever it is."

Barton knew very well what had happened. He knew that I had worked hard with the boys for more than a year now. Ever since he had fired me from the police force. What he didn't know was how I had worked — that the cockfights every Saturday night were the reason that the gangs were getting along. If he had known he would have reported me on the spot.

The day before the parade Lieutenant Simpson stopped me in the hall.

"I hear from the chief that you don't want protection."

"The less, the better," I said.

"What if there's trouble?"

"That'll be the time to call for help."

Lieutenant Simpson had a sharp nose. It reminded me of a bird's beak. He stood with his feet together, stiff as a bird, and pointed his beaklike nose at me.

"That's how good men get killed," he said. "Waiting around and letting things happen. I say let's have plenty of men stationed along the route. Let the Chicanos see that we mean business. Scare the hell out of them."

"It's not going to be much of a parade if we scare hell out of them."

"It's not going to be a parade if we don't," Lieutenant Simpson said.

I was surprised that Simpson had stopped to talk about the parade. He usually didn't discuss anything connected with Probation. It made me uncomfortable. It emphasized the fact that I was out on a limb. In the beginning all I was supposed to do was to furnish the gangs, so to speak, and guarantee that they would show up. Now I was being asked to guarantee that they would behave themselves. I was in for big trouble if they didn't.

"What about Ernie Sierra?" Simpson asked.

"What about him?"

"Are you counting on him for the parade?"

"Sure. Why not?"

Simpson had an ash on his cigaret. He walked down the hall and flicked it into an ashtray and returned.

"I may pick Sierra up, is all," he said. "Maybe tomorrow. So if you have any big plans for him, you'd better change them."

I doubted very much that he had the evidence to arrest Ernie Sierra. He was feeling me out, trying to learn if I knew anything about Sierra that he didn't know.

"It won't make any difference to his gang," I said. "They'll ride in the parade anyway. Sierra or no."

Simpson waited for me to say more, but I played it cool and said nothing. The ash on his cigaret grew again. He walked down the hall, flicked it into the ashtray, and came back.

"How often do you see Ernie Sierra?" he asked me.

"Three times a month."

"When was the last time?"

"About a week ago."

"Did you find out anything?"

"What do you mean?"

"Did you see or hear anything that made you suspicious?"

"About what?"

"Reds. Hash. Marijuana, acid, heroin. The garage down there is a front."

"They're good mechanics," I said. "They do good work."

"They're handling dope."

"If you think that," I said, "why don't you raid them?"

Simpson didn't answer my question. But after a moment he said, "How often do you see your parolees?"

"At least once a month."

"But you see Ernie Sierra three times a month. Why do you see him three times oftener than you see the others?"

"There are others I see three times a month. Four or five others, in fact."

"But three times a month is unusual. You'll have to admit that. What's so unusual about Sierra?"

I was still playing it cool. I was volunteering nothing. "He seems to be making an effort to go straight," I said.

"But you think he may not make it. So you see him often. Keep an eyeball on him. What's he doing that makes you so suspicious? What worries you so much that you check on him three times a month?"

"We've had him up for car theft. He's been in the Joint for assault. For attempted rape. Ernie Sierra is high risk. Strictly high risk."

"Why don't you let him go? Let him get himself in the big Joint? That'll save you a lot of time and worry."

101

Simpson waited for me to answer, but I didn't see any reason to.

"Did Ernie tell you about the money he got?" Simpson asked. "About all the money he inherited from his aunt in Tepic? He didn't tell me, but I heard about it through the grapevine."

"I heard it, too."

"Do you believe Sierra? That the money was left to him?"

"Yes."

"I don't. And I didn't," Simpson said. "I called Tepic and found out that his aunt died, all right. But she didn't leave any money. She died poor. She was a charity case. Had to be buried by the city."

I was surprised but I took pains not to show it.

"He has several aunts," I said. "Three that I know about. One in Mazatlán. One in Tepic. And one in Navajoa. I can get their names for you."

"Don't bother," Simpson said.

His cigaret had another long ash and he walked down the hall and put it in the ashtray. For some reason he didn't come back.

Lieutenant Simpson had been very thorough about the aunt in Tepic. He had gone to more trouble, he had done much better than I had, which didn't make me feel any too good. I was pretty sure that Ernie was a liar, but Simpson had proved it. Still, I was one step ahead of him.

Next day the parade began to assemble at noon and I got all the gangs in the right cars and the cars in the right places. I had worried about Yvonne. Whether she would come with Manuel or Ernie. I expected trouble either way. But she didn't come at all, saying that she had to work, which may have been the truth.

The committee wanted me to ride at the head of the parade with the mayor. I declined the honor because I was afraid of being conspicuous. The boys all knew me and most of them liked me, but I still represented Anglo authority. I was the law, "The Man." Furthermore, Chief Barton and Lieutenant Simpson would not have been overjoyed at the sight of a PO, a parole agent, riding up front with the mayor.

The parade rolled away promptly at two. It would stretch out for a mile and a half, just the length of Main Street. There were four bands — three from the local schools, one from the navy. Between the bands were girl drill squads and baton twirlers. Sandwiched among the teams and twirlers were the automobiles filled with the Mar Vista gangs and their girl friends.

Main Street was lined ten deep. The crowd was much bigger than Mar Vista could turn out, so people must have come in from everywhere along the border. They saw a good parade — lots of music and marching and baton twirling. But if they came to see a gang fight — and I am sure that a lot of them did — they were disappointed. Riding along in the sleek cars, the gangs looked like a bunch of choir boys. And that's the way they behaved, like shining-faced choir boys.

The best thing in the parade — at least to my way of thinking — was Manuel and his Conquistadores. They brought up the rear astride twelve horses. All of the horses were wild mustangs they had captured in Mexico, driven north across the border, and broken at Los Tres Gavilanes Rojos.

Manuel rode in the lead on a small, lively stepping horse. He was dressed in seventeenth-century armor — the kind the conquistadores wore — a helmet with visor and cock feathers, throatlatch and breast plate, knee guards and spurs. The fact that the armor was made of aluminum foil mounted on cardboard made little difference to me or the crowd. From the curb, from a distance of fifty feet, he looked real. As Coronado might have looked on the morning he set out to search for the Seven Golden Cities of Cíbola.

Main Street is almost two miles long, but the side streets don't amount to much, so the parade marched to where Main Street ends, then turned around and marched back. This gave the crowd double its money's worth. Like an instant replay on TV.

But I was glad when the parade was over and all the Chicanos and Chicanas reluctantly climbed out of the shining cars and went back to their barrios. I hung around the station late, for three hours after the parade ended, just in case something happened. But there wasn't a whisper, not a complaint of any kind.

Chief Barton came in and complimented me on what I had done and said that it was the quietest Saturday since he had been in Mar Vista. It was the first time he had ever paid me a compliment so I felt good about the whole thing. Everything had worked out. It looked as if we were going to have a quiet Christmas. But as things turned out, I was wrong. Dead wrong.

16

It started off simple enough. On Thursday evening of the following week Manuel came by the house with two of his friends and asked me if I would like to go to a big barbecue and cockfight down in Mexico.

"It's the biggest this year," he said. "All the gangs are going. And there'll be a big crowd from all over."

"Where?" I asked him.

"Just across the border. About fifteen miles from Tijuana. East. A place called Las Palmas. Nobody lives there now. It used to be a place where fat people went to get themselves thin. But now it's deserted."

I feel about cockfights the same way I feel about bullfights. I like to read about them sometimes.

"The roosters are illegal in Mexico like here in the U.S.," I said.

"Not so much," Manuel replied.

"Very little," Manuel's friend, Chuchu Carrasco, said.

"Not at all," explained Pedie Palomares, the other

friend. "You give the cops a little money and they come and help you with the chickens. They carry the crates and all that stuff."

Manuel and his friends stayed for supper and when they left I promised to be at Los Gavilanes early on Saturday morning.

Alice didn't think much of the idea. "American parole officer arrested in raid on Mexican cockfights," she said. "I can see the headlines."

"There's a chance," I admitted. "But I can't very well turn down the invitation. The Conquistadores are the top gang in my district. It's the first time, the only time, they've ever invited me to go anywhere."

"How about the other gangs?" Alice said. "How are they going to feel if you go as a guest of the Conquistadores?"

"That's already taken care of. Manuel has talked to the other gangs. So it's a general invitation from all of them."

"But you're going with the Conquistadores. What do the Owls think of that?"

"It's all taken care of. I go to the cockfights — wherever they are — with the Conquistadores and come back with the Owls."

"I don't like the whole idea," Alice said. "I don't like cockfighting and I don't like you being mixed up in it."

"Don't forget," I said, "that Abe Lincoln was once a cockpit referee. When he was a young lawyer in Illinois."

"I still don't like the idea," Alice said. "I feel uneasy about it."

I felt a little uneasy myself, but early Saturday morning I started off in good spirits for Los Tres Gavilanes Rojos.

It was another pretty day. The Coronados were floating clear and blue above the sea more than thirty miles away and the mountains of Mexico looked as if you could put a hand out and touch them.

But the freeways were already crowded. In another hour they would be bumper to bumper and you wouldn't be able to see either the islands or the mountains. Sometimes I wish we would have a good teeth-rattling earthquake here along the border. The kind that would scare a half-million people and send them scurrying back where they came from. It would solve the smog problem; a lot of other problems, too.

After I turned off on the road to Los Tres Gavilanes Rojos I passed the old man with the goats. He waved his stick at me and I backed up and stopped the car.

"*Buenos días*," he called in his thin voice, and he came over to the car and peered at me from under his sombrero. "You come often these days," he said, putting a friendly hand on my arm.

108

"Today I'm going with Manuel to the cockfights."

"My grandson," he said.

"I thought so. You look alike."

The old man laughed. "Sixty years ago we looked alike very much."

"You don't go to the fights," I said.

"No more, Señor. But the cocks Manuel takes to Las Palmas today are the descendants of the cocks I owned long ago. We used to fight them here on the ranch in those days. That was before the laws, Señor."

The goats were beginning to nibble at my tires, so I started the motor.

"My name is Delaney," I said.

The old man said, "My name is Saturnino de Lagos y Castillo."

I said goodbye to Saturnino — he was pleased when I called him Don Saturnino — and, scattering the goats, went down the road to the gate at Los Tres Gavilanes Rojos.

There were two beaten-up cars standing outside the gate and I pulled up beside them and parked. The dogs came to the gate, sniffed at me through the slats, but didn't bark.

Manuel's mother came out to greet me. She had on a red dress and red shoes and came tripping down the path in spite of the fact that she was very fat. She stood at the gate for a while and smiled at me until she could catch her breath.

"I am happy, Señor Delaney, that you go to Las Palmas," she said. "You must keep an eye on Manuel and see that he does not get into trouble down there."

I promised her to do what I could and followed her along the weed-grown path that led past the ancient fig tree. Walking in her wake, in a cloud of perfume, was a little suffocating.

"Manuel is crazy about gambling his money," she said. "He is like his grandfather. His grandfather, Don Saturnino, gambled one hundred acres of land on a cockfight. And he lost. _Qué lástima._"

"Yes, what a shame," I said, wondering if it was Don Saturnino who had sold five acres for a pair of riding gloves.

"But Manuel has no land to gamble away," she said. "He has only a little money, Señor. Thirty dollars I gave him. And thirty dollars his grandfather gave him and eight dollars his sister gave him. How much is that? Sixty-eight dollars. That is all. I hope that you caution him to bet wisely."

A rooster began to crow.

"Cortez," Manuel's mother proudly announced. "A good sign, Señor. He only crows when he is angry and wants to fight."

It was a slow, stringy sound that came forth from

110

Cortez' throat. Not an angry sound at all. To me it wasn't much of a sign.

Manuel had put the big red rooster in a crate and was fastening the crate on the back of a horse. The gang — ten of them — were standing around watching him buckle and cinch down the straps. I knew all the boys by name but had had dealings only with Pedie Palomares. One by one they came over and shook hands, without saying anything, and wondering, I guess, why I was there. I was wondering the same thing myself.

Pedie Palomares led a horse over and handed me the reins.

"She is very gentle, Señor," he said.

A couple of the boys laughed at this remark and I swung up into the saddle not knowing what to expect.

Manuel's mother ran over and peered into the coop that held Cortez. He looked out at her, at all of us, with an angry red eye. It has been said by some observers of animals that there is nothing that exceeds the cold ferocity of a hen's gaze. Whoever he was, he had never looked into the gaze of a fighting cock.

Manuel's mother said to him, "Do not forget the blessing, Manuel. You won't, will you? You will obey me?"

Manuel said, "I will obey you, Mama," climbed into the saddle, made a wide gesture with his arm, and shouted, "*Vámonos*."

In single file with Manuel riding up front and leading the horse that carried the two wicker cages, we trotted out the gate and headed south. After a mile we came to a place where our trail met another trail coming down from the north. There was a big sycamore growing at the fork and under it was a small shrine.

Manuel dismounted, took Cortez out of his cage, and asked us to get down and kneel at the shrine.

According to Manuel, his great-great-grandfather had built the shrine long ago, in the year 1850. It was a simple structure of four posts, a back wall, and a slanting roof. In a niche on the wall was a wooden figure of Saint Martin, the patron saint of gamblers. He was about two feet tall, carved of wood, and painted brown. The statue had been stolen many times, Manuel said, but a new one was always put up in his place.

Manuel held the red gamecock up high so Saint Martin could get a good view of him. "Bless Cortez," Manuel said. "Give him great strength and courage so that, like Hernando Cortez, he will win great victories."

Manuel had to break off his prayer because the rooster had freed one leg and was slashing away with it. Luckily his spurs were cut down to stubs, ready for the steel spurs to be fastened on, or he would have done some damage. His yellow, red-rimmed eyes glared at the figure of Saint Martin.

"*Vámonos*," Manuel said. "Let's go before he wears himself out."

He put Cortez back in his wicker cage, threw a cloth over the cage, and we rode on toward Las Palmas.

17

We rode through country that was scattered with cactus and in an hour we reached a small stream. We followed the stream into a canyon that had high red walls and soon came to a defile that opened into a grassy meadow. In the center of the meadow were a lot of buildings and rows of parked cars. There must have been two hundred cars parked around the meadow.

Beyond the buildings were large clumps of palm trees, the kind with long feathery leaves. Apparently they gave the place its name of Las Palmas.

We rode over to the trees and pegged out the horses on long tethers. The grass was knee-deep here and very green. There must have been springs underneath for the grass to be so lush. In spite of the abandoned buildings and piles of rubble it was a beautiful place.

The cockpit was set up in a patio between two wings of a large building. It was about twenty feet square and enclosed by strips of red canvas. The canvas partitions were decorated with pictures of cockfights and scenes from a cattle roundup. Around the pit on three sides were bleachers made of rough planks five tiers high.

The whole thing looked as if it could be knocked down, loaded onto a truck, and carted away in ten minutes' time. But now there were at least five hundred people crowded into the bleachers and more standing around the pit. The din was enough to split your head.

There was a gate on one side of the patio and two gatemen were selling tickets, making change out of their hats that lay on the ground. Manuel and Pedie Palomares showed them the three gamecocks in their coops and went in free. The rest of us had to pay two dollars, which was to be used for prize money.

The first thing I did was to locate the Owls. They had come early by car and had good seats in the top tier. There were more than a dozen of them and they sat squeezed together in a row, dressed in brown caps and brown sweaters.

Pedie Palomares spotted them as soon as I did. "*Mira*," he said, "the Owls. They look like a flock of brown birds sitting on a limb."

It was a good description but not a very good beginning to the day.

The other three gangs were scattered around through the bleachers. The fights hadn't started yet so I made a point of talking to some of the boys from each gang, letting them know that I wasn't playing favorites.

115

At noon someone blew a bugle and the fights started. The first four were between chickens that belonged to a captain in the Mexican army and chickens owned by a cocker from Tijuana. There was heavy betting on all of the fights, but none of the gang members bet. They were saving their money for the fifth match, which would pit a Conquistadores gamecock against a cock owned by the Owls. This was to be a hack fought at a weight of five pounds.

There was heavy gambling on the first four hacks. Gamblers stood at the pit and took bets from the crowd, using hand signals to show the odds and the amount wagered.

The first three fights ran long and it was past two before the fifth fight was announced by a flat-nosed little man wearing a big hat. I had found a seat in the second row where I had a close-up view of the pit, the handlers, and the coops of gamecocks that were arranged in aisles and protected from the hot sun by canvas.

Both of the birds in the fifth fight were Spanish Crosses, cocks with dark plumage and large curving tails. They both came in at the weight of five pounds and they could have been twin brothers, they were so much alike. But Lightning, owned by the Owls, had fought four times, while Chubasco, owned by the Conquistadores, had never fought. The gamblers, therefore, favored the experienced bird at odds of four to one.

Manuel was squatting beside the coop that held Cortez. He had his wide-brimmed hat in his hand and was fanning his prize bird. When Lightning and Chubasco were carried to the pit, I saw him make a motion to one of the gamblers for a wager of thirty dollars.

If he won at the odds he would be ahead by one hundred and twenty dollars. But to me it seemed like a long gamble — two birds of the same weight, of the same stock, but one having the great advantage of experience. I remembered what Manuel's mother had said to me. But that's all I could do — just remember it.

When the two cocks were placed at the judge's command of "Pit," Lightning was slow at the start, a second slow. Chubasco flew straight up, beating its wings, and came down upon Lightning's back. With his first slash he caught a spur in his enemy's wing.

"Handle," the judge shouted. "Twenty seconds."

It took the full time for Pedie Palomares, who was handling Chubasco, to get his spurs untangled.

"Pit," the judge shouted.

This time the two birds got off to an even start. They met in midair, but again Chubasco slashed at his enemy's wing, bowled him over, and was in the air ready for another slash. Lightning, in a great flutter of feathers, suddenly flew from the pit, over the canvas barrier, and disappeared beneath the bleachers. He had had enough. His handlers chased after him, finally caught up with him, but the bird was disqualified by the judge.

Ernie Sierra appeared from somewhere, grabbed the bedraggled gamecock, walked over to the nearest wall, and smashed its head against the bricks.

"We feed no cowards," he said to Pedie Palomares.

The next hack was between two more Spanish Crosses. The betting was even on this one and Manuel put up all of the one hundred and twenty dollars he had won on Chubasco. If I had been betting I would have drawn down half and bet the other half. But Manuel was not cautious — not about betting or anything else.

This hack lasted for almost an hour and went to twelve pittings, with the Conquistadores' gamecock winning again.

Up in the last tier, the Owls were restless and glum. They had lost two of the fights, one in a cowardly fashion. On the other hand, the Conquistadores, sitting behind me, flapped their arms like roosters. They cupped their hands over their mouths and crowed the triumphant crows of victorious fighting cocks.

I didn't think much of the crowing and wing-flapping. It seemed to me that it would have been better if they let the cocks do the strutting. And yet they had been holding cockfights for almost a year now, probably hurling insults at each other just like these, and on every occasion without a scare or a rumble. Whatever the cockfights did for the gangs, whatever the psychology was, it had worked.

I noticed for the first time as I glanced at the silent row of Owls that Ernie Sierra wasn't among them. I finally located him on the far side of the pit, sitting with Yvonne who looked very pretty in a pink pantsuit and a cap with a pink visor.

Ernie hadn't handled the first two cocks the Owls had entered, so I concluded that he knew nothing about the game. But when the next hack was announced, he jumped to his feet and took charge. It was possible he knew that the first two birds had little chance of winning, that he didn't want to handle a pair of losers. At least, not while Yvonne was watching.

18

Betting was brisk on the sixth fight, the big fight between Cortez and Montezuma; so heavy, in fact, that the judge delayed the start for ten minutes to give everyone a chance to place a bet.

The odds began at even money when the fight was announced, but changed quickly when the gamecocks were weighed in. Cortez weighed in at one ounce over the limit.

Manuel stared at the scales. He picked Cortez up and put him down again. The scales still read one ounce too heavy.

"*Qué pasa?*" he said to Pedie Palomares. "Where does the weight come from? He weighed correctly at the ranch."

The judge said, "Your scales, maybe they are incorrect."

"Begging your pardon, Señor, the scales are not incorrect," Manuel said.

"How about if someone gives him a drink?" Pedie Palomares said. He turned and looked at Ernie Sierra who stood a few feet away, holding Montezuma. "How about if one of our friends gives him a few kernels of corn?"

"Do you know someone who would do a chicken thing like that?" Manuel asked.

Pedie Palomares went on staring at Sierra. "Yes," he said, "I know several of these *vatos locos*."

Vato loco in Spanish means a rustic, a simpleton; but it also means more. It is an insult.

Ernie Sierra acted as if he hadn't heard the remark. "Let's get with it," he said to the judge.

"What do you propose?" the judge asked Manuel. "You have five minutes."

Manuel picked up the bird and said something to Pedie Palomares, who disappeared.

Meanwhile the odds changed from even money to three to two in favor of Montezuma. At this point Manuel placed three hundred dollars on Cortez.

Pedie came running back with a leather bag. He took out a pair of dubbing scissors and handed them to Manuel.

Cortez had a heavy shawl of glossy black feathers that formed a shield across his neck and shoulders. Running his fingers under the edge of the shawl, Manuel lifted it and carefully cut away a single row of feathers. He re-

121

peated this operation and cut away three rows. Then he put the cock on the scales.

"Half an ounce over," the judge announced.

Manuel cut the half ounce out of Cortez' tail, one long feather at a time, until the bird was practically tailless.

The odds rose to three and a half to two. The Owls came alive. They shouted insults at the tailless rooster. The Conquistadores shouted back about Lightning, the cobarde that had run away and hidden under the bleachers.

Manuel laid out his gaff case. From the six gaffs in the case he chose a pair two inches long. Cortez' own spurs were already trimmed down to stubs. Manuel cleaned the stubs with his handkerchief and fitted chamois-skin coverings tightly over each one. Then he forced the sockets of the two-inch spurs over the stubs and tied them there carefully with waxed string.

"Twenty-minute time limit or kill?" the man with the flat nose asked Manuel.

"Kill," Manuel said.

He asked Ernie Sierra the same question.

"Kill," Ernie answered.

The judge, who was also acting as referee, examined each of the gamecocks. He checked to see that they hadn't been soaped or peppered and that combs and wattles and earlaps had been properly trimmed. He handled the birds with great care. The tips of the fine-tempered steel spurs were as sharp as needles. And Ernie Sierra and Manuel took the same care when they got the birds back.

"Get ready," the referee said.

Ernie lit a cigaret and blew smoke into his bird's face, two slow lingering puffs. This is supposed to make a cock angry and it did. Montezuma opened his beak, snapped it shut two or three times, and tried to lift his wings.

"Bill your cocks," the referee said.

Manuel and Ernie Sierra stood sidewise to each other, cradling the birds over their left arms. The birds started pecking at each other instantly and kept at it for a full minute. The two boys crouched there silently, not looking at each other, but their anger was plain, as fierce as the anger of the pecking gamecocks.

"Get ready," the referee said again.

The two boys backed away from each other until they reached the chalk lines, which were about three steps apart. They knelt on one knee and held their gamecocks in their right hands, about a foot from the floor.

"Pit!" shouted the referee.

At the same half-second, Manuel and Ernie dropped their birds. But Ernie gave his a slight push, which the referee didn't see. It was an unfair advantage for Montezuma, and he used it to get above Cortez.

In a flash Montezuma hooked the gaff on his left leg into Cortez' wing. Cortez fell on one side, righted himself, but the gaff still stuck to his wingbone.

The Owls from their high perch in the bleachers set up a howl of delight, crowed, and flapped their arms.

"Handle!" the judge said.

At the same time Manuel and Ernie Sierra picked up their gamecocks. Manuel took his time and pulled the gaff free from Cortez' wing. Then they faced each other again at the chalk marks, cradling the cocks, readying them for a second pitting.

Manuel said, "I did not like what you did before. Giving your bird a push."

"You are not the referee," Ernie said. "Let him decide what I do."

"If you push your bird again," Manuel said, "I will decide. If you do any other thing that is unfair, I will decide."

"You talk a lot," Ernie said. "It is too bad your bird is not a parrot. He would learn a lot of words from you."

The two boys were not looking at each other as they spoke. And they spoke quietly, in a tone that made me uneasy.

"Pit," shouted the referee.

This time, as Manuel dropped him cleanly on the floor, Cortez rose into the air, wings beating so fast they were a black blur. His yellow legs churned the air. He landed behind Montezuma a foot or more but the other bird whirled before he could attack and faced him.

There with outstretched necks they froze. They watched each other from a squatting position for a moment, then warily began to move in a circle. Suddenly Cortez rushed out at Montezuma and struck him savagely in the chest. Twice? Three times? It was hard to tell how many times the needle-sharp gaffs struck Montezuma.

Blood began to show on the feathers of his gray shawl, gathered and dropped on the cement floor.

He backed against the barrier and stood there crouching with his neck outstretched. Cortez watched him, but seemed content to bide his time. The bleachers grew restless. Gamblers moved among the crowd shouting new odds. The odds now favored Cortez.

The time limit came with the birds still squared off. The referee commanded Manuel and Ernie Sierra to handle them for the third pitting. Battles between well-matched birds sometimes went as long as twenty pittings. I doubted that this one would go half that number.

19

The third pitting was the last.

Montezuma had suffered an injury to his breastbone. It was nothing fatal but he had lost blood and his dubbed comb grew pale. Ernie blew hard on his back, spat into his open beak, stretched his neck and carefully massaged his thighs. Manuel straightened Cortez' bedraggled tail feathers but did nothing else.

"Get ready," the judge said. "Pit!"

Holding Cortez in both hands, Manuel released him just a fraction of a second before the command. The referee must have seen the move, but for some reason he didn't call it.

With this small advantage, Cortez rushed forward for two or three steps, flew straight up in the air for five feet, trying to get above his opponent. Montezuma at the same moment rushed to one side, out of the reach of the descending spurs, and the two cocks faced each other breast to breast and began to push.

It looked for a moment as if they would have to be

handled again. But suddenly Montezuma raised his hackles, fluttered the tips of his wings, and jumped high off the concrete floor. As Cortez feinted to his right in a quick move, a descending gaff caught his left eye.

The blow stunned him. He staggered to one side against the barrier, fell on his back and tried to right himself. It looked as if his brain had been injured by the gaff. Grown confident at the sight of his struggling enemy, Montezuma pressed in upon him. He began to peck at his enemy's bleeding head.

There was a lot of noise but I could hear the Owls yelling behind me, and a shriek that I recognized as coming from Yvonne. Which bird she was shrieking for I couldn't tell.

This new pain aroused Cortez, I guess, for he fanned his wings and managed to get on his feet. He stood there for a while shaking the blood from his eyes. Then he walked away from Montezuma a few slow steps. Then he whirled in a circle and I thought he meant to fly out of the pit. But suddenly he leaped in the air, straight up, and as he came down caught Montezuma with two hard blows on the spine. This effort seemed to exhaust him. He crouched against the floor and began to take long gasping breaths.

Montezuma lay on his side, his legs sprawled out at a queer angle, two feet away. Cortez moved toward him, close enough to reach out and give him a peck on the head. Then Cortez drew his neck back and waited. He never moved his one red-rimmed eye away from the enemy. He was confident that he had strength enough left for another final blow.

Both gamecocks were dying. But who would be the first to die? The crowd was quiet. The boys were on their knees at opposite sides of the pit. The referee looked at his watch and waited. There were still a few minutes to go before the time limit was up.

Montezuma kicked one leg and lay quiet. The referee went over and picked him up and held him limp for a moment. Then he motioned to Ernie that his gamecock was dead.

Ernie took Montezuma by the feet and walked over to the pile of dead chickens and tossed him into the pile. Then he picked up Yvonne and they left, or at least I didn't see them again that day. The row of Owls disappeared, too.

Manuel lifted Cortez from the floor and wiped the blood from his head and straightened out his feathers. Pedie Palomares brought the coop and they put Cortez in it and hung a blanket over the coop.

Manuel seemed to be more concerned about Cortez than the money he had won. I left him when the gamblers were paying him off and went looking for someone in the other three gangs to take me back to Mar Vista. All the gangs had gone, including the Owls, so I returned to the pit and helped Manuel get the coops ready to take home.

It was about midafternoon by the time Manuel had gathered up the rest of the Conquistadores. We took the coops out to the meadow and Manuel sent two of the boys out to bring up the horses. They came running back in a few minutes with the news that the horses were gone.

All of us started running across the meadow toward the grove of palm trees where we had tethered the horses. It was half a mile away.

The horses were gone, all right. The stakes we had set were gone and also the ropes that were fastened to them were gone. Whoever had stampeded our horses had not taken the time to untie them. They had simply pulled up the stakes and driven the horses away.

"What do you think?" Pedie Palomares said. "Someone stole them?"

"No," Manuel said, pointing to tire marks in the heavy grass. "They drove a car up here, pulled up the stakes, and spooked the horses."

"Who do you think would do that?" Pedie wanted to know.

"I don't think," Manuel said. "Who else would do it but the Owls?"

I expected to see him in a rage, but he stood there calmly looking at the tire marks.

"*Vatas cobardes,*" Pedie said, stomping back and forth.

The rest of the gang joined him in cursing the Owls.

"I'll cut their hearts out," Pedie said and the rest joined him in his threat, except Manuel.

"Shut up. All of you!" Manuel said.

He may have said this to impress me. After all, I was the one who would try to prevent them from fighting the Owls. And the one who would throw them in jail if they did fight. But I don't think so. I think his anger was too deep for threats.

The hoof marks of the horses showed plain in the grass. There were tire marks on both sides of the hoof prints. Whoever it was had driven the horses through the palm grove and out the other side.

On the far side of the grove the tire marks turned back upon themselves. Manuel and Pedie Palomares ran on ahead of us in that direction for about a hundred yards. There they stopped.

They were pointing down when we came up. They stood on the edge, the very brink, of a cliff. The cliff was sheared off, as if by a great knife, and plunged straight down into a tumble of rocks and pine trees. Spread over a small area, as if they all had plunged to their deaths at once, were our horses, two of them impaled upon dead limbs, the rest scattered among the trees.

Nobody spoke. There were no curses or threats. We backed away from the cliff in silence. We went through the grove and across the meadow and picked up the three coops.

"We can go back and hitch a ride," Pedie Palomares said.

"We can walk," Manuel said.

And we did, back along the trail we had come, still in silence, until we came to the little shrine of Saint Martin.

Cortez had died and Manuel lifted him out of the crate and laid him on the ground. We knelt in front of the shrine. Manuel prayed to Saint Martin. He prayed quietly, using only a few words.

"Thank you," he said, "for our victory. And be with us when we encounter our enemies."

Two of the boys dug a hole with their knives and Manuel put Cortez in the hole and covered him over with dirt and two heavy rocks to keep the coyotes out. Then we started off on the short trail to the ranch of The Three Red Hawks.

20

I didn't sleep much Saturday night. I lay awake and thought about the year's hard work that had gone down the drain. I saw the horses lying at the foot of Las Palmas cliff. I remembered Manuel's face as he stood there looking down into the abyss. I heard his words as we knelt in the dust before the wayside shrine: "And be with us when we encounter our enemies."

I tried to keep it from Alice but next morning, half-way through breakfast, I gave in and told her.

She got up from the table, poured coffee for me and herself, and put the pot back on the stove. She looked out the window, watched some kids playing in the street, sat down and drank her coffee. She took a long time to answer.

"I'm glad," she finally said. "Not about the horses, of course. Or the trouble it's going to cause . . ."

"It's going to be big trouble," I said.

"But still I'm glad. I mean, I never did like the idea of the cockfights."

"They prevented a lot of broken heads. Saved a lot of

property. Maybe some lives. You remember all the vandalism at the school."

"I remember," Alice said. "They wrecked my classroom."

"There hasn't been any of that sort of thing in more than a year. And all on account of the cockfights. Instead of destroying things, fighting among themselves, they've let the gamecocks do the fighting."

"Identification, it's called," Alice said. "It's the Owls and the Conquistadores fighting, not the gamecocks."

"And it works," I said.

"But cockfighting's cruel," Alice said. "It's worse than bullfighting. Letting two roosters slash at each other for an hour, sometimes longer, until one of them, or both of them, is slashed to ribbons is deliberately cruel."

"A gamecock's bred and brought up to fight," I said. "He wouldn't know what to do if he didn't fight. He'd probably die of boredom."

"Not being a gamecock, how do you know?"

"I don't need to be a gamecock to know. Besides, a gamecock wouldn't be alive in the first place unless he could fight. Who would spend time and money raising a bird that wouldn't fight?"

"It would be better if he wasn't born and raised," Alice said. "Life isn't meant to be abused that way."

There was some loud talk outside in the street and

133

Alice got up and went to the window to see what was going on. I could have told her that it was Montgomery, our next-door neighbor's son, who is a likely candidate for Juvenile Hall. If his father weren't a city councilman and if he happened to live on the wrong side of the tracks, he'd be in the Hall already.

Alice came back and sat down to finish her coffee. "What can you expect when the Conquistadores win three cockfights in a row?" she asked me. "Naturally the Owls struck back. And they struck back in the same terms as the cockfights. Brutally. How can you expect anything else? You're lucky, to my way of thinking, that there hasn't been a blowup long before this."

"It's a big mess now," I said, feeling more discouraged than I ever had since the first day I started in Probation.

"There's a story that reminds me of your predicament," Alice said. "It's about Lorenzo and Miguel. Lorenzo hated Miguel who lived in a neighboring village. And Miguel hated Lorenzo. On market days whenever they met they stared at each other and muttered bloody threats. One night Lorenzo prayed to God to punish his enemy.

"God said to him, 'I will punish Miguel, as you wish. But I must punish you also, although what I give to you I will give double to your enemy. Think hard, Lorenzo. Tell Me what is the punishment you wish for yourself.

Tell Me so that I may know how to punish Miguel.'

"Thinking hard, Lorenzo raised his face to God and said, 'Tear out one of my eyes!' "

"What's all that got to do with me?" I asked.

"You're dealing with the same situation," Alice said, "only you have fifty Miguels and Lorenzos."

I wasn't in much of a mood for a debate. All hell was going to break loose and my problem was to stop it. Not to talk about it.

My guess was that Ernie Sierra and his Owls had stampeded the horses. There were plenty of reasons to think so. The long-time feud between the two gangs, for one thing. The rivalry between Manuel and Ernie Sierra, for another. The victory of Cortez over the Owls' Montezuma. And Ernie Sierra himself — a tough, hard-headed kid from the mountain jungles of Michoacan where they must raise their kids on tiger milk.

I didn't have to worry about Ernie Sierra at the moment. The trouble, when it came, would come from Manuel and the Conquistadores.

I was supposed to take Alice to church, but I ducked out and drove down to Los Tres Gavilanes Rojos, losing no time getting there. It was a fog-bound morning around Mar Vista but the sky cleared as I went south and I was there well before noon.

Don Saturnino was tending his goats in the grassy swale where I had met him before. I stopped the car and waited for him to come over. He greeted me warmly and asked what he could do for me — just name my wish, he would endeavor to fulfill it.

"I'm looking for Manuel," I told him.

"He is gone to Las Palmas," the old man said. "He took my stallion and left last night before supper."

"Did he tell you about the horses?"

"Yes, he explained."

"Who does he think did it?" I hadn't talked to Manuel at all yesterday afternoon when we got back. He was too mad to talk and I didn't ask him.

"He is not sure," Don Saturnino said. "But he will find out."

"I'd like to talk to him before he does."

"It will be to no purpose, Señor, for you to talk to him. He stands where he is. He has taken a stand. That is where he is now, standing."

"It's that bad?"

"Bad, Señor. Bad."

"There's nothing to say?"

"*Nada*," the old man said. "I would do the same. I would stand there, like he stands. When I was young, I stood many times."

I was up against the code — the macho code. I was wasting breath. The big male goat, who was smelling worse than he had before, started to nibble at my radiator.

"When do you look for Manuel?" I asked.

The old man shrugged his shoulders. "Who knows? Maybe today. Maybe tomorrow."

"*Adiós*," I said.

"*Adiós, amigo*. And may God go with you."

As I drove away, I prayed that He would.

At the first filling station I called Lieutenant Morales in Tijuana and made a date to meet him at the bull-fights. I had talked to Morales in the middle of the week, but he was busy, the connection was poor, and I learned nothing except that he was still working on el problema, as he called it, of Ernie Sierra.

I learned little more from him at the bullring that afternoon. Between fights I gave him what I knew about Sierra. From my own observations and from what Lieutenant Simpson had said. He added nothing to the picture. But he did give me some advice about Paco Chacon.

"Remember," Morales said, "he's the half cousin of *loco en la cabeza*."

"You gave Manuel a message for him."

"Yes. He is the one in the green Chevy with two big fat tires on the rear. If you see him and Ernie Sierra together riding around in the green Chevy with the big fat tires, do not hesitate. Descend on them. *Immediatamente*. You will have an answer to *el problema*, perhaps."

I didn't wait until the fights were over, but left early. Morales walked out to the gate with me.

"You did not take the advice," he said. "You still fool around with the drugs. It is dirty business. I like you, Señor. I wish you would not fool around with the drugs."

On my way home I stopped at El Sombrero Café on the chance that Yvonne would be on duty. She was there, behind the counter, looking pretty in a golden wig with a lot of curls down the sides. She smiled her quick now-you-see-it-now-you-don't smile, but didn't seem especially glad that I had dropped by.

I ordered a cup of coffee and when she brought it I said, "Too bad about Manuel's horses."

"I heard about them," she said.

"Who did it?" I asked her.

"How would I know?"

"You were with Ernie."

She wiped up some of the coffee she had just spilled on the counter. "But Ernie didn't do it," she said.

"If he didn't, then who did?"

"Probably the Roadrunners."

"Why the Roadrunners?"

"They're a wise-ass bunch."

Two customers came in and sat down across from me and Yvonne went over and took their order. She drifted back while she was waiting for the kitchen to fill the order.

"Manny must have made a bundle on the fights," she said.

"He made a little, I guess."

"He bet on all three fights. And he must have doubled his bets each time. He must have made a thousand dollars. Maybe more."

Before I could answer she went out to the kitchen to pick up orders. The counter was filling up so I put fifty cents on the counter and left.

Fog was coming in from the sea and the first winter lights blinked on as I headed for home. It had been a long day and I hadn't accomplished anything. About the only thing I could remember was Morales' suggestion: If I saw Paco Chacon and Ernie Sierra riding around together in a green Chevy truck with big fat tires on the rear, I was to pull them in *immediatamente!* It had been a bad day.

21

We were fogged in solid on Monday morning, but I managed to get to San Diego by eight, picked up my mail at the office, filled out a report, and was back in Mar Vista by nine thirty. I was moving against time. I had no plan, nothing but a hunch. And a terrible feeling that whatever I did it wouldn't amount to much in the end.

Lieutenant Simpson was just coming on duty when I walked in. I asked if I could see him for a moment and we went into his office. He closed the two windows, fixed the drapes, sat down, and began to sharpen a pencil that was already sharp.

"What can I do for you?" he said without looking up.

"Is there anything new on Ernie Sierra?"

"Nothing. We've had a tail on him for a month. But he's lying low now and we've taken it off."

"What do you mean by lying low?"

"He hasn't been across the border for a couple of weeks."

Simpson put the pencil in a drawer and pulled out a rubberized tobacco pouch. He had given up cigarets and was smoking a pipe with a long, curving stem. He filled the pipe and put the pouch away. I wondered if he was trying to look like Sherlock Holmes. If he was, it occurred to me he had a long way to go.

"I never could figure out why you didn't pick him up," I said. "Sometime when he was over in Mexico."

"We've picked him up twice. Once in Mexico. Once at the border."

"He never told me about it."

"Why should he?"

Simpson's pipe had gone out and he lit it again, blew the match out, broke it in two pieces, and put the pieces carefully in the ashtray.

"What's your theory about Sierra?" I asked. "His part in the operation?"

"He's a courier. The stuff comes from Mexico. It's grown there, probably in Nayarit, and processed there. He picks it up from someone, brings it across the border, and turns it over to someone here."

"He's just responsible for getting it across the line?"

"That's all."

"How do you figure he's handling the stuff?"

"We thought he was using a truck. But both times

we stopped him, we drew a blank. We took the truck apart, piece by piece, down to the chassis. All we found were chicken coops and a lot of feathers."

"He might be walking it across."

"Too risky. With hash or marijuana, yes. But pure Mexican heroin is selling for ten thousand dollars a pound wholesale. Diluted, a pound will concoct thirty thousand shots worth a quarter of a million in the street."

"They could be bringing it by plane."

"They are, some of it. But not with this operation."

"I might have to pick him up today," I said.

Simpson was sucking on his pipe. He took it out of his mouth. "If you pick him up, you'll mess up what we're doing."

"But according to what you just said, you're doing nothing. Just sitting around."

"If you're going to pick up Sierra, you'll have to clear it with Barton."

"I'll tell Chief Barton, but I don't have to clear it. I'm not working for the Mar Vista Police Department."

Simpson pointed his sharp nose at me for a moment but decided to let the challenge drop.

"Why pick up Sierra today? He's been around for a long time. Why today?"

He hadn't heard about the rumble at Las Palmas, apparently, and I decided not to tell him.

"There's trouble shaping up between the gangs," I

explained. "I might be able to head it off by picking up Sierra."

"Hell," Simpson said, "let them fight. Get it out of their systems."

"I might do that," I said.

22

About ten o'clock when I left Lieutenant Simpson's office I drove down to the Sierra garage.

I found Ernie out back in the chicken yard, scattering feed from a pail. He must have heard me drive in, but he went on scattering the feed.

"I looked for you after the cockfights," I said.

He scattered another handful of feed on the ground.

"I planned to bum a ride home," I said.

"I didn't know you wanted a ride. Why didn't you say so?"

"I did."

"When?"

"When I was here last week."

"I don't remember. Too bad. I have a bad memory. But you got home all right."

"Yes. I walked."

He must have known that I had walked, that all of us had walked, but he acted as if it were a great surprise.

"Walked? How come?"

"Because we lost our horses."

"Lost? What do you mean?"

"Someone drove them over the cliff at Las Palmas," I said.

Ernie struck his forehead hard with the palm of his hand. *"Madre de Dios!"* he cried. "Over the cliff? What cliff?"

Ernie was a good actor. He would have done well in a soap opera.

"There's a cliff over east of the meadow where the palms are," I explained, being very cool about it. "It drops down five hundred feet. Straight down and . . ."

"They drove the horses over?" Ernie asked.

"They did," I said. "Do you know anyone who'd do something like that?"

Ernie wrinkled his forehead and thought for a moment. "It might be the Roadrunners. They could do it."

"Why?"

"Because they're *pochos*. *Pochos* do things like that."

Pocho, which means "simpleton" in Spanish, is also the name for anyone born in Tijuana who is now a citizen of the U.S. of A. Pochos are low in the pecking order. The Anglos looked down on the Chicanos. The Chicanos looked down on the pochos. And the pochos looked down on the blacks.

"Remember last year," Ernie said, "the time they put a tie on the railroad track and two cars went off. Boom! Boom!"

Ernie turned the pail over and dumped the rest of the feed on the ground. There were no pigeons around except some squabs with their heads sticking out of the nests. I asked him where they were, the young ones he was teaching to home.

Ernie closed the gate but didn't lock it. His eyes were set deep in his head, like an Indian's. He looked out at me for an instant, thinking something that was way back in his mind.

"My uncle's got the pigeons," Ernie said. "He took them over to Jacumba last night. He's going to let them loose today. Around noon when the fog clears up, I guess. They're not too good in the fog. The last time I had them out in a fog, they got lost. They should have been here in an hour. It took those *locos* three hours to get home."

"Do they ever learn to fly in a fog?" I asked him.

"Sure. They got eyes like radar. They can see through a wall. But these ones, they are young and *muy loco*."

On the way out to my car I noticed a pickup sitting in the garage with the rear end jacked up. It was a green Chevy and had big wide tires on the rear. I recalled as I walked by that on Saturday I had seen wide tracks in the meadow. They ran up near the cliff and turned back. The pickup had wide whitewalls on the rear and they had grass stains on them, the kind of stains you would get if you drove fast through high grass.

"Who belongs to the pickup?" I said.

"Chacon."

"Paco Chacon?"

"Sí."

I suddenly recalled Lieutenant Morales' remarks about Paco Chacon. "If you see him and Ernie Sierra together riding around in a green Chevy with big fat tires, do not hesitate. Descend on them. *Immediatamente.* You will have an answer to *el problema,* perhaps."

Well, here was the green Chevy and Ernie Sierra. The only thing missing was Paco Chacon.

"Was Chacon at the cockfights?" I asked.

"I don't think so," Ernie said. "But I don't know."

"When did he leave the pickup?"

"Last week sometime. Thursday or Friday."

"What's wrong with it?"

"Ignition."

I got in my car and turned on the motor. "There's going to be trouble about the horses," I said. "I'd like to head it off."

"I'll help you. I'll call a meeting right away tonight and talk to the boys. I'll find out who did it. The Roadrunners, *probablemente.*"

"There's going to be trouble about the horses," I said.

"Manuel thinks you and the Owls are responsible. He'll be over this way to talk to you."

"He better come prepared."

"I'd like to head things off," I said. "The way Manuel feels now, somebody's sure to get whacked out."

"We'll do the whacking," Ernie said. "Tell him and his gang to stay away if they don't want to lose their ears."

"I'm not in touch with Manuel," I said.

Ernie was short and weighed about one hundred and sixty. He looked like a walking tree stump.

"I don't know where Manuel is. But you're here and I'm going to take you in."

Ernie backed up a step and for an instant I thought he was going to make a run for it.

"You can't bust me for Las Palmas," he said. He took another step backward.

"This has nothing to do with Las Palmas. I think you stampeded the horses, but that's not why I am taking you in."

"Why? What's the idea? *Qué pasa?*"

"I'll tell you later. When we get to the Hall."

I wasn't sure he would go. By regulation a PO is not allowed to carry a hand gun. So I didn't have one. I was no match for him physically and more than likely he was carrying a switchblade.

"Let's go," I said.

"I've got to do something in the house. I've got water boiling. I have to turn it off."

"Now," I said. "*Vámonos.*"

He hung back. "What about my pigeons?"

"Your uncle will take care of the pigeons."

I was doing a foolish thing, picking up a tough kid without help. I should have had an officer with a pair of handcuffs and a gun backing me up. That was routine in this sort of situation — a strong backup. But there wasn't any time to go to a phone and call for help. If I did, knowing Sierra, I was sure that he would be gone when I got back.

"What's the big idea?" he said. "I don't get it."

I dug deep for a reason. "I guess you know that Manuel blames you for the stampede."

"I didn't do it. I already told you once."

"It doesn't matter. The point is, Manuel and his gang think you did. I was out to Los Gavilanes yesterday and I got the idea that Manuel would be coming down this way."

"Let him come," Sierra said. "I will have his ears."

"He could come today. This morning."

"I am ready."

"There'll be a fight," I said.

"I'm not going to duck out."

"You won't be ducking," I said. "I'm taking you in.

You have nothing to do with it. I'm the one who's responsible, not you."

Sierra flicked his eyes toward the house, then toward the pigeon loft.

"You can make a run for it," I said. "But if you do, I'll call the station and get help. We'll catch up with you wherever you are and bring you back."

He took a deep breath, filled his chest, then followed me to the car. I still expected him to bolt or pull a knife from somewhere. But he didn't do either one. He got into the car and carefully fastened the seatbelt. Of all things, the seatbelt.

23

It was only fifteen minutes by freeway to Juvenile Hall, but it was going to be a long ride.

I took the quickest route to the freeway, which was down Main Street. This took me past the police station. There was still time to stop and pick up an officer. I could even leave Sierra at the station and put a hold on him. But either way meant that Simpson and Chief Barton would want to know what I was up to.

When we passed the station, Sierra said, "Hey, man, I thought I was going here."

"You want to?" I said, trying to make a joke out of it. "You have friends you want to see?"

"Where we going?" he said.

"Downtown."

"Juvenile?"

"Yes."

I left Main Street and got onto the freeway and set the speedometer at 60. The speed limit was 70 but I didn't want Sierra to think that I was in any hurry.

"What goes on at Juvenile?" he said.

"Same old thing," I said.

"With me, I mean."

"Like I said, I want you off the street for a couple of days. Manuel Castillo will be cruising around looking for trouble. I'll catch up with him today or tomorrow and try to cool him off."

"I could save you the trouble," Sierra said. "I'll cool him off good."

He was quiet for a while, sitting there with the belt tight, staring out the window. But every minute that went by I half-expected him to flash a blade and hold it against my ribs. He'd do this quietly so no one would notice. Then he'd tell me to drive off the freeway and down some country road. There he'd either stick the blade under my ribs, up in front, very gently (he told me once that sticking a knife into someone's heart was just like sticking a knife into butter — very soft); he'd either do that or toss me out, take the car, and head for Mexico.

"It's a bummer," Ernie said and kept repeating the words softly to himself.

I really think that one thing or the other would have happened if it hadn't been for Motorcycle Officer Kincaid. When I was turning off the freeway he came up beside me.

"What's new?" he yelled.

"Nothing much," I answered, but I gave him a wink that told him something.

Anyway, instead of passing, he fell back and tailed me all the way to Juvenile Hall. (I thanked him later for saving my life, which was a surprise to him.)

Sierra gave me and the sergeant a bad time — he was familiar with all his rights and all the legalities — but we finally got him booked on a temporary hold for parole violation. Which meant that I would have to come up with a charge within seventy-two hours or have him released.

I was back in Mar Vista before noon. I went out to the Sierra garage to take a good look at the green Chevy.

I verified the grass stains on the whitewalls and found that the truck had a broken left spring. I was standing there beside the truck when I heard a noise coming from the driveway, a jingle of spurs and the thud of hoofs.

It was Manuel on a gray pony, riding with a long-barreled musket across his lap.

He didn't recognize me at first. He must have taken me for Ernie's uncle for he raised the musket and held it, ready to fire.

I walked out of the shadow of the garage and spoke to him.

"Who's around?" he asked me.

"Nobody," I said and told him about Ernie Sierra. "But his uncle will be along, anytime now."

"I'll wait," Manuel said.

He slipped the musket into the leather sheath and jumped down from his horse. The musket must have belonged to his great-grandfather, it was so old and battered.

"I don't want you to wait around," I told him. "I've got Ernie stashed away for safekeeping. And I'll put you away, too. Somewhere. There'll be no shooting."

"I'll just talk to Ernie's uncle."

"Ernie's uncle hasn't anything to do with the horses," I said. "You can't hold him to blame for what Ernie did. If he did it."

"He did it, all right. I can prove it."

At that moment, there was a whir of wings over our heads. A flock of pigeons made a circle of the loft, then flew lower and settled on two perches that ran the length of the loft. There were about three dozen of them and they all, one after the other, floated down to the ground and drank out of a tub, standing on the edge, dipping their beaks, and holding their heads back. They must have flown in from a long distance, for they all drank for a long time.

"I used to have homers," Manuel said. "Homers and brown tumblers and fantails. But I liked the homers best. I used to take them up in the mountains and let them go and then try to beat them home. But I never did beat them."

I watched the last of the pigeons balancing itself on the edge of the tub. Its legs were a bright pink, I guess from all the exertion of flying a long distance. Like the rest, it was banded.

"I used to send messages, too," Manuel said. "I read about how they sent messages that way during the war. Secret messages. I used to send messages to my sisters. I'd write something down on a piece of paper and fasten it to the band on a pigeon's leg. My sisters always got my messages. Except once when two hunters killed my whole flock as it was flying past."

As I stood there watching the pigeon drink and half-listening to Manuel, an odd thought came to me. But it really wasn't a thought. It wasn't that strong. It was more like the shadow of a thought.

"I never owned any pigeons," I said. "I lived in town where it was against the law. I suppose you could send a lot of different things by pigeons."

"Anything that wasn't too heavy," Manuel said. "Anything they could carry."

"How much could they carry? In weight, I mean."

"I don't know. Not much."

The door to the loft wasn't locked. I opened it and went in and closed the door. The loft was dark with stripes of light coming through the cracks. There was a wide wooden strip on hinges and I let this down, which closed the loft.

I reached up and caught one of the pigeons. It was still hot from its long flight. I opened the loft door and closed it behind me.

"Hold its wings," I said to Manuel. "I want to take a look at the band."

"It's larger than the ones I used," Manuel said. He took the pigeon in his two hands and stretched its leg out so I could examine the band.

The band was made of very thin aluminum. It was about three-eighths of an inch wide and fit loosely on the pigeon's leg. There was a small pin on one side and when I took it out a tiny gate came open. The two parts of the band were hollow, and as I turned them over in my hand what looked like brown sugar fell out into my palm.

"Crazy," Manuel said. "What is it?"

"Mexican heroin," I said. "Uncut, probably."

"Uncut?"

"Not diluted." I spread the heroin gently out on my palm. "It feels and looks like pure stuff."

I stood there for a moment staring. Then I scraped the heroin back into the band as best I could, closed the tiny gate and slipped the pin in place, and put the band in my pocket.

I carried the pigeon back to the loft, closed the door, and Manuel and I started off through the yard toward my car.

Then I remembered that Ernie Sierra had asked me if he could go into the house to turn off the gas. At least this is what he had said. Not out of kindness or consideration so much as plain curiosity, I hurriedly retraced my steps and went into the kitchen. There was no water, no fire on the two-burner stove.

I didn't tarry. At any moment Carlos Sierra would be here and I didn't want to be around when he came. As I closed the kitchen door I heard a car go past the house. I couldn't see it from where I stood but Manuel was watching it.

"Paco Chacon," Manuel said. "He is going to the end of the street. At the freeway he will turn back because he has to. He will see my horse and come in maybe. He is making the turn now."

Manuel spoke slowly, reporting what he saw without any interest. He wasn't much concerned about Chacon or the heroin I had found, either one. He was thinking only about Ernie and Carlos Sierra and the musket he had brought along to use on both of them.

"Listen, Manuel," I said. "Listen carefully."

I took hold of his arm and clamped down on it hard until he looked at me.

"Listen to what I say. There are two phones, one in the garage and one in the house. Go in the house and phone the Mar Vista police station. The number is two-four-two, three-three-six-three. If you forget the number, dial 0 and tell the operator it's an emergency and to get you the police station. Tell whoever answers that I'm here at Sierra's garage and that I'm in trouble. Tell them to hurry."

Manuel repeated the number to himself and went in the house. Paco Chacon made a slow turn into the driveway, then speeded up as he saw me, and came to a grinding halt in front of the garage.

24

The Sierra garage was on a dead-end street. It was dead-end because Freeway 92 had cut it off right in the middle. At one time there had been some pretty good houses on the street, but since the freeway came through the Anglos had moved out and a lot of poor Chicanos had moved in. The yards were heaped up with old tires, cars without wheels, rusty bedsprings, and beaten-up bicycles.

The Sierra garage was jammed up against the freeway on one side, and on the other side stood an abandoned junk yard. Across the street were a couple of acres overgrown with weeds and dusty castor bean trees. There was no one within shouting distance in any direction.

It was an isolated spot on an isolated street. As things turned out that day, this was the real reason the garage was there and that it was owned by Carlos Sierra.

I hadn't thought about this isolation when Paco Chacon drove down the street. Or when he parked the car and got out. Or when his leather jacket hiked up and I saw that he was carrying a gun strapped to his shoulder. But I thought about it hard as I walked along with the band filled with heroin in my coat pocket.

I reached the garage before Chacon saw me. To my surprise he raised his hand in what seemed like a friendly greeting, but said nothing and disappeared into the garage.

The phone was located at the front of the garage beside a window that looked out toward the house. Chacon headed straight for the phone and picked up the receiver. I was standing less than ten feet from him and I could hear a sound on the line. Whether it was the sound of a voice or of someone dialing, I couldn't tell. It could be Manuel on the line, either calling the police or talking to them. On the other hand, it was a party line, so anyone in the area could be making a call or receiving one.

Chacon began to dial. He dialed slowly with a pause between each number, blotting out the sounds. Then he stopped and listened for a moment. Then he muffled the receiver against his chest and glared at me.

"Is Manny on the phone?" he said.

"I don't know," I answered. "He could be. He's in the house."

Keeping his eyes on me, Chacon put the receiver to his ear and started to dial. Again I heard the sounds on the phone. One of the big transports boomed past on the freeway and I couldn't hear anything. There was a longshoremen's strike going on in L.A. harbor and they were unloading ships at Ensenada and the transports were trucking the cargoes across the border.

Then there was silence and Chacon said to someone at the other end, "What number do you have there? Two-four-two, three-three-six-three? Sorry, I got the wrong number." He hung up the phone and waited.

To me 242-3363 was a familiar number. It belonged to the Mar Vista Police Department. Manuel had reached the police. The question was, had he had a chance to give them my message?

It was quiet again. All I could hear was the pigeons cooing far away in the loft. Then the phone rang. Chacon picked up the receiver. He listened and then turned to me.

"It's Ernie and he's at Juvenile Hall. He wants to talk to Carlos."

"Tell him his uncle isn't here," I said. "Tell him that Carlos will call him when he gets here."

By regulations, Ernie Sierra was allowed to make one call to his parents or guardian.

The kitchen door opened and closed. I saw Manuel go down the steps. He walked toward the gray pony. He looked calm, as if he were out for a stroll. He reached up and slipped the battered musket from its sheath. His movements were all slow and deliberate.

161

Paco Chacon turned his back on the phone, facing me. He was tall and gaunt, with lips that stuck out.

He smiled and took a step forward. "I am Paco Chacon, Manuel's cousin," he said, and thrust out a hand in greeting.

I took it, unthinking. His grip was firm. As I returned it, bony fingers clamped down upon my hand and I was suddenly yanked forward off my feet. I was trying to recover my balance when he reached under his coat with his free hand.

It was all very quick. I saw the blue of a gun. I felt a dull blow against my skull. The blow blinded me for a moment and I fell to the ground. The ground was covered with grease and I slid under the green Chevy that was up on jacks and came out the other side, with the truck between me and Chacon.

Crouching there I could see Manuel standing in front of his gray pony, holding the old musket against his shoulder, not more than fifty feet away. I could see Chacon's boots pointing out, away from me. I was close to him, lying there on the ground, but I was helpless.

There was a heavy car spring lying beside me and I picked it up. It was a good weapon in a hand-to-hand fight; in fact it was the most popular of all weapons in a gang fight. Next to a tire chain. But it wasn't a good weapon against a gun, especially the gun that I had seen strapped to Chacon's ribs.

By reaching out under the jacked-up truck I could give Chacon a blow with the car spring. But it would not be a hard blow, not hard enough to keep him from stooping down and shooting me square between the eyes.

I crouched there holding the greasy weapon. A big transport was booming by on the freeway. Then there was a quiet spell for a few moments, and I could hear pigeons cooing softly in the far off loft.

Manuel called, "Drop the gun, Cousin Paco."

Chacon shifted his weight from one foot to the other, but he didn't drop the gun.

Crouching, I backed away along the side of the truck. I stayed low and kept both men within sight.

"Cousin Paco," Manuel called again. "I beg of you to drop the gun. You are a no-good, but drop the gun."

A transport was thundering past as Chacon's gun went off. The shot sounded feeble against the thunder of the big truck. But the bullet spun Manuel around. He stumbled sidewise, fell to one knee, still holding his musket.

Chacon ran toward the front of the truck. He was headed for his car. I noticed for the first time that he had left his engine running. I swung the car spring and caught him a glancing blow on the shoulder.

The blow surprised him. Turning his head, he acted stunned as if he didn't know where the blow had come from. Then he saw me crouching behind the fender, shifted his weight, and fired. The bullet made a hot noise close to my head, bounced off the hood of the truck, and went out with a clatter through the tin siding of the garage.

Manuel's shot caught Paco Chacon in the back. It was an old musket and it fired a single ball, but it killed Chacon as quickly as a shotgun blast.

25

The papers made a big thing of it. They ran headlines like "Largest Heroin Haul in Years Made by Mar Vista Authorities." "Parole Officer Hero of Heroin Shootout." And they sent a photographer over and wanted to take a picture of me standing in front of the Sierra garage with a car spring in my hand. They even sent a photographer over to the hospital and took a picture of Manuel with his leg held up in a sling and a cute Chicana nurse smiling down at him.

It was all embarrassing for a while. Sometimes in my high school days I had dreamed of getting my picture on the front page. But now that it had happened I felt embarrassed. It also made things pretty uncomfortable at home and at the station.

Especially at the station. Chief Barton took the whole thing in stride and even paid me a compliment or two. But the state let me know that parole officers were not hired to track down drug dealers. I think they would have fired me if they had thought they could get away with it.

Lieutenant Simpson was the worst, however. He didn't say much, but he was convinced, from what I heard, that I was trying to ease him out and get my old detective job back.

When I dropped by the Mar Vista office and met him in the hall or somewhere, he always had a smart crack for me.

"What do you hear from the Mafia?" was one of his favorites. He also liked, "What's the price of heroin if I bring my own container?" The one that really bothered me was about Carlos Sierra. Sierra had gotten wind of us at the garage and had escaped across the border.

Simpson would ask, "How's your friend Carlos Sierra these days?"

He wanted me to know that if he had been handling the raid he wouldn't have let Sierra get away.

But it was Manuel being in the hospital that bothered me the most. Although he had come over to the garage to start a fight with Ernie Sierra, I felt responsible for his getting shot. I could have told him simply to jump on his horse and go home. And if I had been satisfied with just putting Sierra away in Juvenile Hall, everything would have worked out fine, too.

Still, it was lucky the way it turned out. Manuel could

have been killed. As it was, he had only a flesh wound and stayed in the hospital for less than a week.

I didn't get up to see him every day, but I did manage every other day. I met Yvonne twice when I was there. Manuel didn't think much of the hospital food, so she brought him a sack full of tacos and burritos every time. Now that Ernie was in Juvenile Hall and would go to Deuell or Preston and be gone for a long time, she was concentrating on Manuel.

She didn't have much to say to me. For one thing, I think she blamed me for getting Manuel shot. For another, she must have realized that I didn't like her and that I'd influence Manuel if I could.

I took Manny home just before Christmas and helped the family out a little with some presents. Then, because I had been neglecting my other boys, I didn't see him for almost a month.

I went out to the ranch after I got a call from him that he wanted to talk to me and one from Miss Stokes at the high school. She wanted to know when I thought Manuel would be ready to come back to school. I was surprised, because he should have been ready right after Christmas.

I drove out to Los Tres Gavilanes Rojos the next day. The skies were a greenish yellow and it was raining off and on, with a strong wind blowing in from the southeast.

Manny was braiding some leather strips into a halter for his pony. We sat in the living room talking — his mother, Manuel, and I — in front of a fire. I didn't bring up the school matter until I had been there a while.

"I'm not going back," Manny said.

"He's got better things to do," his mother explained.

"I don't know about that," Manny said. "But I just don't want to. I've got too much work to make up."

"They'll give you a break on that," I said. "Miss Stokes told me that they'll make things easy for you until you catch up."

"I don't want things easy."

"You were doing fine work," I said. "Miss Stokes told me."

Manny wouldn't say any more, so I didn't press things, thinking that I'd come back to it again, sometime soon when his mother wasn't around.

I left during a letup in the rain and Manuel followed me out to the car. He didn't say anything until I got in the car and turned on the motor.

Then he said, "Mr. Delaney, you're my friend. You've been good to me."

"I got you shot," I said. "Almost killed."

He grinned — at what, I don't know. Then he said, "Mr. Delaney, I'm in trouble."

"That's human," I said. "It happens all the time with people."

"It's like this. You know Yvonne? Well, she's in trouble. She's pregnant. She's going to have a child."

I turned off the motor. It had started to rain again. I told him to get in the car.

"Thank you," he said and got in.

"You're the father?"

"Yes."

I felt like saying, "How do you know you're the father? How about Ernie?"

"What are you going to do?" I said.

"I want to marry her, but she doesn't think it's a good idea. On account of me not having a job. She wants to get a doctor to fix her so she won't have anything."

I sat there and watched the rain beating against the windshield. I didn't know what to say. Manny was in love with this girl; that was clear from the way he looked at me. It was in his eyes and in his voice. I sat there and watched the rain come down.

"She wanted money for the doctor," Manuel said. "Three hundred dollars. I didn't want to give it to her, but she said that if I didn't, she wouldn't speak to me, ever. We were finished, forever."

"You gave her the money?"

"I didn't want to. But I did."

"When?"

"Yesterday. She came out here and I gave her the money."

"Three hundred dollars?"

"Yes."

"Do you think it would do any good if I talked to her?"

"Yes. That's why I wanted to see you."

I think he felt better about things by the time I left. Anyway, I did the best I could do, which wasn't much.

The rain increased and the dry watercourses were beginning to fill up as I drove away from the ranch. By the time I got to the Sombrero Café, water was running over the curbs. It was noon and Yvonne wasn't there and wouldn't be until five.

At five I went back and by luck caught the place when it was empty. Yvonne was polishing the big shining pressure machine. She always seemed to be doing this, so I guess she liked to.

She spoke as I sat down at the counter, but didn't come over until she had finished with the polishing. Sitting there, I remembered that the last time I had seen her was the day after the cockfights and she had mentioned the fact that Manuel had made a lot of money on the fights.

"I've been talking to Manuel," I said when she came over to take my order. "I've just been out to the ranch. He tells me you're pregnant. He says you're going to have an abortion."

She gave me a flicking glance and began to polish the

sugar bowl that was sitting in front of me. "It's none of your business what I am," she said. "You're always snooping around. Sticking your nose in other people's affairs. Well, let me tell you something, wise guy, stay out of mine."

"You don't need to pay a doctor three hundred for an abortion," I said. "There's a good county referral service and you can go down there and it'll cost you only one hundred and twenty-five."

"I don't want any county welfare deal," Yvonne said. "I want my own doctor."

"It's not welfare," I said. "You have to pay."

I hadn't ordered yet and she asked me what I wanted.

"Coffee and a jelly doughnut," I said.

She went away and came back with my order. Then she picked up the sugar bowl again and began to polish it. She looked calmer now.

She stretched her neck, as if the gold and bead necklace she wore was too tight. She looked tired. It was a tiring job to be on your feet all day, running back and forth with armloads of heavy dishes, smelling fried grease and leftover food, listening to gripes from cranky customers. For a moment I felt sorry for her.

"Ernie's finally made the big league," I said. "He's been trying to get up there for a long time and now he's made it."

"What's Ernie got to do with me?" Yvonne asked.

171

"What? Well, if you don't watch your step you're going to make the big league, too."

"Meaning?"

"Meaning," I said, "that unless you hand back the three hundred dollars that Manuel handed you, I'll have to do something."

Yvonne's eyes suddenly filled with fury.

"How would you like to have this sugar bowl bounced off your head?" she asked me.

"I wouldn't like it," I said, "and you wouldn't like it either."

I got on my feet, moving my head out of the way.

Yvonne put the sugar bowl down. She gave me a blank stare. Her eyes were pale in the harsh light. Then there came into them a puzzled, frightened look. It told me, as clearly as if she had written it down on the counter, that I had guessed right.

"I'll be back tomorrow to get the three hundred dollars," I said.

26

I got the three hundred dollars back the next day, and toward the end of the week I took it out to Tres Gavilanes. On the way I tried to think of something to say when I gave the money to Manuel.

But what do you say to a young man when you tell him that a girl he's in love with is a cheat? Do you say, "You're young and you'll get over it"? Or "There're more fish in the sea than have ever been caught"? Or "There's a pretty girl on our street and I'll introduce you"?

Manuel was out in the corral watching his fighting cocks when I got there. I needn't have worried over what to say. He climbed over the corral gate, held his hand out stiffly, and smiled. The only sign that something was wrong was when he started to speak. He carefully framed each word and his lips moved silently, before he could say anything.

"My big gray has just hatched nine eggs," he said. "Nine out of nine. That's a record."

"I'd like to see them," I said.

"She's rattled now. Maybe she'll settle down before you go. She's a very nervous hen."

We stood looking at each other for a while. Then Manny began to frame his words again.

"I hitched a ride down there the other day," he said. "The day before yesterday. I saw Yvonne but I couldn't get her to talk. So I stayed around until the next morning and went back. That was yesterday, and she was working. I waited around for her to talk to me. I drank a lot of Cokes and waited around until noon. Then she talked a little. But she was mad and didn't say much."

"Did she say that she gave me the money?"

"Yes, that's the last thing she said."

I handed him the three hundred dollars and he stuffed them in his Levis without looking.

I had a few words that I thought of saying, but I didn't say them. The rains had brought on the first sprouts of winter grass and we talked for a while about grazing prospects. Then we went in the chicken house, he lifted up the big gray hen, and showed me the nine chicks.

"When I get back here," Manny said, "they'll be old enough to train."

"Back from where?"

"Yesterday afternoon I signed up with the *Sinbad*. She's going down to Panama to fish for tuna."

My first reaction to this news was disappointment.

"What about school? You're going to give up?" I asked him.

"There's nothing to give up."

"How about the Conquistadores? What's going to happen to them?"

"They'll get along. They'll elect a new president and everything'll be fine. Now that Ernie Sierra's out of the way, everything will run along good."

I smiled and tried to look enthusiastic. "You'll make some money down in Panama."

"I never thought about that," Manuel said.

And the way he said it made me feel that he hadn't thought about it.

"Tuna are bringing better than five hundred dollars a ton in San Diego. I read it in the paper last night. You'll get a share of the catch."

"I guess so."

"Be sure it's in your contract."

He reached in his back pocket and pulled out a piece of paper and handed it to me. The contract was written in ink, properly dated and signed, but I saw at a glance that he was hired on only as a hand.

"You don't get a share of the catch," I explained. "You get a wage and your food, nothing else."

"*No importa*," he said.

There were a few fishermen around the harbor that

lived by taking advantage of young Chicanos, and it made me mad.

"I'll talk to the captain of the *Sinbad*," I said.

And I did, the day Manuel sailed. The captain was a handsome young Mexican named Salazar, sailing under the flag of Panama which gave him a right to avoid a lot of the responsibilities he'd have under the American flag. One of these was the Panamanian privilege of underpaying his crew.

"By this contract," I said, waving the paper in front of him, "you're paying the boy a dollar an hour, when he works."

"Correct, Señor," the captain said.

"It isn't close to a minimum wage."

"He has no experience, Señor. He has never been on a boat before. He's not worth a dollar. Maybe half a dollar."

"And he only gets a dollar an hour when he's fishing."

"But he will fish a lot, Señor. He will make a lot of money. He will have no place to spend the money. He will come home *muy rico*. Besides, Señor, he gets all the food free. No charge for the food, Señor."

Manuel was standing by, shifting from one foot to the other, afraid that I was going to mess things up for him. I'm sure he would have gone aboard if he'd been paid nothing for his work.

"How about twenty cents an hour more," I said in a final effort.

"No, Señor," the captain said firmly. "It is impossible. Next time, yes. This time, it is *imposible*."

The *Sinbad* was an eighty footer with a high prow and a fantail stern. According to what I learned from friends on the waterfront, she was built in 1910 and had been in a couple of wrecks off of Baja California. She looked as if she'd been in a dozen.

Sinbad was supposed to sail at noon, but something went wrong with the main pump on the refrigeration. Then the pump was fixed but three of the crew were missing. At five they came stumbling on, three shaggy derelicts drunk to the eyeballs.

I drove up on Point Loma and parked the car and watched *Sinbad* sailing out. The sun was down but there was still a glow on the water. I watched the rusty old tub until she rounded Coronado Reef and headed south for Panama. I hoped that she'd make it. Standing up there on the headland with the wind blowing cold and the great Pacific swells coming in, I hoped that Manuel would make it, too.

27

I kept track of the *Sinbad*. We have good marine reports in our local newspaper, both from the U.S. and the Mexican coastguard, because the owner of the paper, John Lambert, is the owner of three tuna clippers. Mr. Lambert gets regular reports from his ships and passes them along a couple of times a week in a column called "At Sea."

The first report I read was that *Sinbad* had weathered a storm off San José del Cabo and reached Mazatlán safely. She stayed at Mazatlán for three days where she underwent repairs.

Then for more than two weeks there was no news of *Sinbad*. She wasn't sighted. She wasn't in touch with anyone on ship-to-shore radio. She was as silent as if she had dropped off the edge of the world.

A few days later "At Sea" ran a disturbing item relayed from one of Lambert's clippers:

Guayaquil, Ecuador, February 2.

A navy gunboat today picked up the vessel *Sinbad* ten miles off Cabo San Lorenzo. She was thought to be fishing illegally at the time of seizure in waters belonging to Ecuador, but upon boarding her, it was discovered that she was adrift and that her crew had mutinied and was holding the captain prisoner. The ship was towed into port this morning and the crew released to Ecuadorian civil authorities.

I can truthfully say that I wasn't surprised by this turn of events.

Sinbad was certainly a rusty, worm-eaten tub. Her ancient diesels would be hard to start and harder still to keep running. In any sort of sea she would wallow and pitch and leak at every seam. Her pumps would need to work half of every day to keep her afloat. That she'd broken down, therefore, and gone adrift on the wild coast of Ecuador was logical.

I'd seen very little of her handsome young captain before *Sinbad* sailed out from San Diego. But I'd seen enough to tell me that he would be a tough taskmaster. He would work his crew until the men dropped. He would feed them weevily food and scant the rations. He would try to cheat them out of their honest wages. That finally he would drive them to mutiny seemed to be a good possibility.

179

I called the newspaper. I talked to the reporter who wrote the news column and asked him if there was any information about *Sinbad* that he hadn't published. There was none, he told me, but if something came in he would call me right away.

I talked to Lieutenant Morales in Tijuana and learned that he had no connections in Guayaquil. I called the Mexican consul in San Diego who suggested that I call the American consul in Guayaquil.

I didn't get the consul but I did get an assistant of some sort. He knew about the case, and said that he was doing all he could to see that the Americans involved were free on bond. Any chances of talking to Manuel on the phone, which I had thought about, were small, he said. "Don't waste your money," was the way he put it.

Three days later the local reporter called me early in the morning. He had just talked to the captain of one of Lambert's tuna boats. The captain, who was in Guayaquil to take on water, had heard that the trial of the five Americans was scheduled to take place the following day and that the chances of four of the five Americans going free, according to gossip along the waterfront, were excellent. But the fifth American, Manuel Castillo, who was considered the leader of the mutiny, would be found guilty and sent to prison.

This was upsetting news. South American prisons

were notorious — men who didn't die within their walls often wished that they would.

The call from the newspaper came while Alice and I were eating breakfast. I told her all I had just heard on the phone.

"Wouldn't you know," I said, "that of all the crew it was Manuel who led the mutiny?"

"Yes, I would know," Alice said. "It's no surprise. Maybe to you, but not to me."

"There's nothing I can do," I said. "I'm powerless. Manuel's on his own now."

"That's good," Alice said, with her mouth full of toast. "Before this, there's always been someone around to bail him out."

28

Meanwhile, during the time I was worrying about Manuel Castillo, I gathered some new responsibilities. My department had sent home more than a hundred boys at Christmas time and of these I got my share. Nine, to be exact, which gave me a load of fifty all together. Luckily, I no longer had Ernie Sierra to worry about. Since he was equal to about a dozen ordinary parolees the load wasn't as big as it looked.

But I had a fine candidate for Sierra's place as my number one headache. His name was Mondo Martinez.

Martinez had been sent up a month or two before I joined the agency on a marijuana charge. He was a quiet boy with a pale face and a lot of hair and I thought he wasn't very bright the first time I talked to him.

Inside a month I changed my mind. The first sign of his activities came from a neighborhood in Mar Vista where he lived with his father, who was a gardener. People began to lose their garden hoses. Then other people in other parts of the town lost hoses. Then people lost garden tools and a farmer on the outskirts of Mar Vista lost a tractor — a big, bulldozing tractor driven away while the owner was absent.

The police saved me a lot of trouble. They discovered that Mondo Martinez had driven the tractor to a canyon near the freeway, bulldozed off a level plot, and planted it to marijuana. The garden hoses he had stolen were fastened together, connected to a fire hydrant two miles away — imagine, two miles of garden hose — belonging to the fire department, and used to water his growing plants.

I was sorry to see him go back to Deuell. His ingenuity deserved a much better fate.

Our gangs had started the new year peacefully enough, with Manuel gone from the Conquistadores and Sierra from the Owls. The two gangs elected different leaders, made a few noises, yet behaved themselves generally. The other three gangs, who always imitated the Owls and the Conquistadores, trailed along.

But early in May things changed suddenly.

The town of Mar Vista was started by John Lambert's grandfather, Roy Rollins Lambert. Grandfather Lambert was raised in Pennsylvania and came to California during the Civil War.

Mar Vista was just a name then, a general store on a dusty road surrounded by some small valleys and a range of hills where cattle roamed. There was a depression on at the time and a drought so bad that steers were selling for twenty cents a head. Land was dirt cheap, too. Grandfather Lambert bought three thousand acres of it, five hundred acres from Los Tres Gavilanes Rojos, for five dollars and twenty cents an acre.

Grandfather Lambert raised cattle on his ranch, sold out the cattle, and ran sheep because sheep did better on poor pasture than cattle. Then he sold off the sheep, planted wine grapes — four hundred acres of vines he imported all the way from France — and started a winery.

In 1909, the year Grandfather Lambert died, disease struck the vineyard. All the vines withered away, the winery was shut down and abandoned. Forty years passed, then his grandson replanted the vineyard, using disease-free stock, and the winery started up again.

From the beginning there had always been a colony of Mexicans living on the ranch — in a barrio called La Cresta — doing work with the cattle, then the sheep, then the grapes. After the vineyard was abandoned they stayed on in their barrio and did work around the town. When the winery started up again, they began to work again in the vineyard. There were more than a hundred families living in La Cresta now, most of them born there in the barrio.

The trouble started with a rumor. The vines at La Cresta had just leafed out and the grapes were only the size of buckshot, but word went around that Lambert was thinking about using a mechanical picker at harvest time.

John Lambert was noted for his new ideas. He had revolutionized the tuna fleet by shifting from boats that caught tuna one at a time on jack poles to fast-moving purse seiners that scooped up ten tons in a single set. His canneries also were very modern and efficient. His newspapers were efficient, too.

I first heard about the mechanical grape pickers when I went to La Cresta to see a couple of my parolees. All the men in the barrio were talking about it. The women were silent and looked scared and the children looked scared because of their mothers.

Gonzales, who was the man everyone listened to in the barrio, said, "I haven't seen one of these things. But I hear they can pick more grapes in a day than fifty men."

"I haven't seen one either," his son said. "But these new machines are full of bugs. They break down a lot and right in the middle of the harvest."

"They straddle the rows. They go along and grab everything in sight," Gonzales said.

"They bruise the grapes bad," the son of Gonzales said.

"We're all out of luck if the big machine comes," Gonzales said.

185

"We can go on welfare," the son said.

I had read about the grape-picking machine. I knew that it was already being used in the vineyards of the Central Valley up north and was very successful there. Thinking about it, I wondered why Lambert hadn't brought it in long before this.

When I went out to La Cresta again in about two weeks they were still talking about the big machine with the steel fingers that picked more grapes in a day than fifty men could. And the women were still scared and the children were silent.

29

The first news I had from Manuel, after the news about the trial, came in April from the captain of one of Lambert's ships. He was unloading tuna in San Diego and he called me to give me a message.

The message had been given to him six weeks before from the prison at Guayaquil. Manuel was behind bars, serving a five-year sentence for his part in the mutiny. He wanted me to know that he was feeling fine, the captain said, and that he'd be seeing me soon.

There was something odd about the remark that struck me. Manny was serving a five-year sentence in a South American prison and yet his message was that he'd be seeing me soon. Obviously, he was planning to make an escape. And he was not only planning an escape, but he was also confident that he'd be successful.

I was not surprised, therefore, when he arrived in the harbor on a tuna boat, called and casually said that he was home. I wasn't so surprised as I was relieved. To tell the truth, I was greatly relieved.

"The hard part," he told me next day when he came over to the office, "was getting out of Guayaquil. The prison part was easy. I had one hundred dollars that I won at the cockfights. I had it folded up tight and braided into my hair. In the back where it's thick. I knew I could make it out when I sent the message to you. One of the guards told me that he would get me out for fifty dollars. That's a lot of money down there in Ecuador."

"Like a couple of months' pay," I said.

"More, maybe three months'," Manny said. "Anyway, the guard said he would get me out. His name was Sanchez, Pablo Sanchez. But he would have to wait for the right time to spring me. That was when the kitchen got through with a barrel of lard they were using up. All the prisoners got a piece of lard every day to use on their bread. It didn't taste very good but it was better than nothing. I checked about the barrel of lard every time I had kitchen duty. About once a week. They only passed out a tablespoon of lard at a meal for each man. There was an awful lot of lard in that barrel. It took two months to empty.

"The guard told me the day I would be going. I was to save bread from my supper and be in the kitchen early. I did as he told me. I saved two slices of bread and was in the kitchen at dawn when the cooks started to work. After I mopped up the floor I went outside where we kept the garbage. Sanchez was there and told me to climb in the empty lard barrel that was standing by the kitchen door. I climbed in and he dumped three big buckets full of garbage — potato peels, banana skins, greasy leftovers — in on top of me. He put the lid on the barrel and pushed it down hard. Sanchez was very careful. He left a piece of potato peel hanging outside."

I sat with my mouth open, listening. It was like listening to someone reading out of an adventure book.

"Sanchez had things all worked out," Manny said. "In just a few minutes the garbage cart came and the two garbage men picked the barrel up and set it down in the cart. One of the men said that it was very heavy and the other one told him to shut up. They drove on and picked up two more barrels. Then the cart went out the prison gate and bumped along for a long time, maybe an hour. I had made a little air hole with my fingers so I could breathe through it. It was awful hot in the barrel because my head was buried under the garbage.

"Then we came to a place where they dumped the garbage and the men emptied the cart. The dump place was in a small canyon and when they pushed the barrel out it went rolling down and then it hit hard against the bottom. I got thrown out when it hit. All around me was a big pile of garbage. All around the edges of the pile there were pigs snorting and squealing. They were fighting over the garbage and when one of them saw me lying there it came trotting along in little jerky steps toward me. It had tusks on each side of its mouth. There was a plank lying there by the barrel — it could have been one of the staves — and I picked it up, but the pig took a rush at me and grabbed my arm. I hit it a hard blow on the snout with the plank and it let go. But I got a bad bite out of it."

Manny stopped and rolled up his sleeve. On the inside of his arm from his elbow to his shoulder there were two wide grooves, white and deep, that weren't entirely healed.

"It was just getting light. Sanchez had given me a ragged shirt and a pair of pants cut off at the knees. There were two huts not far away with smoke coming up. But there was nobody around. I took the clothes and my pieces of bread and went down the canyon past the huts. I came to a beach and the sea. I rubbed myself with sand and took a bath. I rubbed myself with sand again and took another bath. The water was warm. It was like warm milk. Then I buried my old shirt and the pants that had stripes on them and put on the clothes Sanchez gave me."

The shirt and trousers Manny was wearing now were too small for him. He must have grown a couple of inches since I had seen him last, but he was still thin. I noticed for the first time that he wasn't hesitating anymore, forming the words with his lips before he spoke as he used to do.

"There were three small boats anchored nearby," Manny went on. "I guess they belonged to the people that lived in the huts. I ate my two pieces of bread and then I swam over to the boats. I decided to take the smallest one. It had a mast not much taller than I am and a torn sail. I had never sailed before but I got the boat moving and headed north toward a point of land. I figured that the city was behind the point somewhere.

"The harbor was just around the point and I got there about noon. It took me a long time to figure out what to do. I pulled down the sail and just sat and figured. I drifted around until the harbor lights came on. There was no wind now, but there was a paddle with a broken handle lying under the seat and I paddled over to where some ships were anchored. The night was very hot and sailors were leaning over the rails. Some of them spoke as I went by. I went around the whole harbor until I came to an American ship. There was no one on deck so I tied up on the anchor chain and lay down and fell asleep. When the first fisherman came on deck in the morning, I asked him if I could talk to the mate about a job. I could tell by the rigging and the big skiff at the stern that the ship was fishing for tuna. I talked to the mate and he gave me a job. Then we left . . ."

Manny quit in the middle of a sentence. He took a breath, got up, and stretched his long legs.

"I've been talking a lot," he said. "I've got to be going. I haven't been home yet."

"I'll give you a lift," I said, although my desk was piled up with work.

30

I heard the rest of Manny's story as we drove to Los Tres Gavilanes Rojos.

Manny got out of the harbor by hiding in a locker in the engine room and then fished for six weeks around the Galapagos and as far south as Chile. Then he signed on with one of Lambert's ships for the return voyage to San Diego. He arrived in San Diego with five dollars and ten cents in his pocket, left from the hundred dollars he had started with. He had worked for only bunk and meals on the two tuna boats. But it was Salazar, the Mexican captain, that he was bitter about.

"He didn't have a regular cook," Manny said. "And all we got to eat was beans. Beans three times a day. And a few tortillas on Sunday. Tortillas out of a can, made in Chicago by some people called the Dubrowski Brothers."

"Sounds *muy malo*."

"*Sí, malo*. We came close to starving. But that is not the worst. We did not get paid. Not one copper *centavo.* Every port we went into, Salazar promised to pay us. San José del Cabo, Mazatlán, Manzanillo, Salina Cruz, Buenaventura, it was all the same. Promises but no money. And how Salazar drove us! *Madre de Dios!* He drove us from one job to the other. He worked us sixteen hours a day just trying to keep the old barge from sinking. She finally did break down and we drifted for three days. We wanted to radio for help but Salazar was afraid he might have to pay a salvage fee if someone picked us up. On the third day, around sunset, I jumped him from behind. He always carried a pistol and I got that away from him and we tied him down. The next morning the Ecuador ship came along and picked us out of the surf."

We were passing La Cresta and there was a big crowd standing beside the road. A bunch of sheriffs' cars were parked along the Madre Zanca, the mother ditch where they ran irrigation water for the vineyard.

I slowed down and Manny waved at some Chicanos he recognized in the crowd.

"*Qué pasa?*" he asked me.

I told him about the workers' fear of being put out of work if Lambert brought in the grape picker.

"I read in the paper last night," I said, "that some workers had beaten up one of Lambert's foremen. It looks like they've called out the county sheriffs."

"What's the picker like?" Manny said.

"I haven't seen it. I guess it's like a cotton picker."

"But how can anything pick grapes? It must pick branches and leaves and everything, not just the grapes."

"Everything, I guess."

Manny opened the door. "Excuse me, Mr. Delaney; I think I'll get out. I want to see the picker. I'm only a mile from home. I'll walk it."

"The picker hasn't come yet," I said. "According to the paper, it won't be here for a couple of days."

Manny got out anyway. He closed the door and thanked me. I turned around and as I headed back to town I turned on the local radio station, thinking that I'd hear some late news about La Cresta. I didn't find anything on the radio and it wasn't until I got home and read the evening paper that I learned that a worker had been shot to death that morning, just after Manny and I had come along.

There was a short editorial in the newspaper signed by John Lambert asking the governor of the state to call out the militia before other men were killed. There was also a picture of the grape picker and an article about how efficient it was and how it would not take jobs away from anyone, but in time would increase the number of workmen La Cresta employed.

"What do you think of the grape picker?" I asked Alice while we were eating supper. "It picks more grapes in a day than a hundred men."

"What do the grapes look like after they're picked?" Alice asked. "I'd think they would be pretty well bruised up."

"La Cresta makes wine out of the grapes, so it wouldn't matter much if they're bruised. What I mean is, what side do you take in the fight — John Lambert's and his picker or the workers'?"

"Anything John Lambert's for," Alice said, "I'm against. It's just that simple."

And that was pretty much the feeling around town. Those who liked Lambert were for the mechanical grape picker and those who didn't like him were for the workmen. Few had any idea whether the picker was any good or not. Some said that it broke the grape skins, and this caused fermentation which gave the wine a funny taste. Others said that it didn't give the wine a funny taste.

But there wasn't any doubt that the picker would throw men and women out of work. On this, everyone seemed to agree, except the evening newspaper and John Lambert.

31

The mechanical grape picker came down from the north two days later.

The newspaper was mysterious about when it would arrive; otherwise there would have been a crowd on Main Street to watch. As things happened, it came early in the morning, with two motorcycle policemen riding out in front and two riding along behind. Between them and the picker were two cars carrying "wide load" signs.

The picker had six rubber-tired wheels, each of them taller than a man, and it took up the beds of a truck and trailer. It was painted red like a fire engine and had a yellow canopy over the seat where the driver sat. The picker went so fast down Main Street that a couple of young Chicanos standing on the corner only had a chance to throw two stones before it disappeared.

The word huelga, which means "strike" in Spanish, had begun to appear around town, scrawled on walls and buildings.

When I dropped by the Mar Vista station that morning, Chief Barton and Lieutenant Simpson were talking outside the front door. It was already hot and they were standing in their shirt sleeves with their coats hanging over their arms.

They hadn't been friendly toward each other since the dope was seized at Sierra's garage. Chief Barton was not open in his criticism of Simpson for being thickheaded about the case, but he was critical and Simpson felt it. The fact that Chief Barton seldom lost a chance to compliment me on my part didn't help things either.

The two men were talking about the best way to handle the La Cresta trouble and they went on as if I weren't there.

"What we have," Chief Barton said, "is a general confrontation. A carload of Brown Berets came in last night and are camped out at La Cresta. They've got a banner strung up on posts. *Viva Atzlan.*"

Atzlan is the name among the Brown Berets and some Chicanos for all the territory the Americans took from the Mexicans in the War of 1846 — the states of California, Arizona, New Mexico, Colorado, and Texas — the whole American Southwest.

"You'd think they'd get behind something like helping the grape pickers keep their jobs," Simpson said. "But no, the brown glue sniffers want half the U.S. They always screw things up. How the hell does Atzlan have anything to do with picking grapes?"

Chief Barton turned to me. "What are the gangs up to?"

"Nothing, so far as I've heard."

"You haven't heard very good then," Simpson said. "Your friend Manuel Castillo is around there trying to strike the winery. The workers don't belong to a union and he's got a bunch of them cornered into painting *Huelga* signs on the wine vats. Cesar Chavez has got some men there, too, scouting around. And, like always, a bunch of commies."

"If you go out, Delaney," Chief Barton said, "you might have a talk with Castillo. Tell him to lay off the *huelga* business. And if you see any other of your boys, tell them to do the same. There'll be trouble enough without the young *huelgistos*."

"Tell them," Simpson said, "to stay away from La Cresta or they'll have their heads busted."

As things turned out, it was good advice he gave me.

I didn't get to La Cresta until around noon. The sun was coming straight down. Everything was baking in the heat. The brown hills and the distant mountains seemed to be on fire.

At the entrance to the winery, where the road turns off, there's a big sign that says, "Welcome to La Cresta.

Come and Sample Our Excellent Wines — Free." The sign was now covered by slogans splashed on in red paint. They were mostly Huelga slogans but there were others like Viva la Raza and Viva Chicanos.

The road from the main road up to the winery, which was surfaced with white gravel, I guess for scenic reasons, glittered like millions of diamonds. On both sides of the glittering road the grape vines sparkled, covered with heavy clusters of green and white grapes.

The road was about a half-mile long and it went straight up from the main road to a big parking place and turn-around in front of the winery. The parking place was filled with cars and trucks and there were a lot of motorcycles parked off by themselves, some with their radios on.

A crowd was milling around in front of the winery. A man in a gray uniform holding a bullhorn stood on the steps outside huge oak doors with a welcome sign above them. The sign had been blotted out by slogans, which were badly painted and hard to read.

The man in the gray uniform was a company guard. He kept walking back and forth in front of the entrance, sweating and mopping his face. Now and then he'd stop and shout through the horn, "*Vámonos.* Let's go. *Vámonos.*"

There was a small fountain to one side of the steps and I went over to get a drink. As I stooped down I heard Manuel's voice. I finished my drink and went over to where he was standing. He was surrounded by a crowd — it looked like all the members of all the gangs in Mar Vista — a hundred Chicanos at least. Some of them had rocks in their hands.

"We go," Manuel shouted. "We go now. Unless we go now we are *patas muertos*. Dead ducks."

Arturo Vega, the new leader of the Owls, shouted that they shouldn't be chickens and run away.

"*Las platas*, the shields," Manuel shouted back, "will kill us all. Kill us dead. Look around; you will see a shield behind every bush. In ten minutes they will have us by the throats."

He started off down the road that shone like diamonds in the blinding sun. A few hung back, but in a moment they too followed him.

The field workers and those who worked in the winery were gathered along the road. They fell in behind the Chicanos and followed them out to the main road and off the La Cresta property. Then two company guards put up a wooden barrier across the road that led up to the winery, blocking it off. And a car filled with sheriffs came up and parked in front of the barrier.

I drove down the road to where the Chicano gangs were standing. All the boys were armed now, with rocks and sticks.

"You're up against the law," I said to them.

"We're always up against the law," Arturo Vega shouted.

Manuel said nothing. He stood off by himself looking out at the vineyard, at row after row of green vines sparkling in the beating sun.

I walked over to him. "You can march up and down the road," I said. "You can carry signs. You can sing and shout. But you can't defy the law. There are a dozen sheriffs watching you and there are a dozen more where they came from. The officers are armed with guns and you are armed with rocks."

Manuel didn't seem to hear me. If he did, there was no sign of it.

"I was thinking about the captain of the *Sinbad*," he said. "How he starved us and cheated us out of what we earned. It makes me mad. I know some of these field workers and I know one man who works in the winery. I have a bad feeling when I think about them losing their jobs. They are mixed up in my mind. Both things are mixed up in my mind together. It makes me very mad to think about them."

"When does the picking start?" I asked Manny.

"I hear it's tomorrow," he said. "They took a sugar test today. They take a test every day for sugar. Tomorrow the grapes have the right amount of sugar, so maybe they will pick."

"I can go your way," I said. "I can drop you off."

"I am going to stay," Manny said. "We've got food and we're going to wait around for a while. Arturo Vega brought his guitar and we'll sleep in the field. Until tomorrow, anyway."

32

I went back to La Cresta at dawn. The sun was coming up hot as I drove down the road and parked near the wooden trestles that blocked off the white road to the winery.

A new squad of sheriffs was coming on duty. They were all carrying shotguns and seemed to be in a happy mood.

The gangs were camped in a dry swale off the main road under a thin sycamore tree. There weren't as many of them as yesterday, about half as many, which struck me as being a hopeful sign. They had a fire going and a couple of pans of tortillas frying. Arturo Vega had a guitar in his lap and was singing a revolutionary song about the rebel hero, Emiliano Zapata.

Manuel was sitting off by himself with his back against a stump. He got up and held out his hand. He was taller now than I was.

"They're going to pick today," he said. "I heard it from a worker friend of mine. They've got the grape picker up there now, he says. He says she's got a big diesel that runs *muy suave*."

The field workers were coming from their barrio, walking in the middle of the road, with their wives, children, and old people. A young girl led the way, carrying an image of the Virgin of Guadalupe. A sheriff with a gun under his arm stopped them at the barrier.

"Three Chavez men came to our camp last night," Manny said. "They brought some food and told us not to fight. If we don't fight they will help us. But three other men came last night and wanted us to fight. They had bombs, Coke bottles with wicks and gasoline in them. 'A truck load of bombs,' they said, 'enough bombs to burn up the vineyard!' 'The vines are green,' I said, 'and they won't burn.' 'The grass around the vines will burn,' they said, 'and the smoke will ruin the grapes.' Arturo Vega and the Owls voted for the bombs, but we voted against the bombs.

" 'If we ruin the vines,' I said to the three men, 'what happens to the workers who prune the vines when the grapes are picked? To my friends, the men and women who take off the grapes when they are growing in the spring next year? What happens to them?'

"The three men left with the bombs. Now Arturo

Vega is sitting over there under the tree, playing his guitar. He is playing and singing and thinking about the bombs. But he is mad and would like to think up something to do. He would like to shoot someone, perhaps."

Manny turned around and yelled at Vega. "Listen, *amigo*. Be careful with what goes on in your head. Think softly about Zapata and sing some more of the good songs. I like the ones of Villa, also. That Pancho Villa. What a man, that Pancho!"

"*Más hombre que tú podrás ser en esta vida.* More man than you'll ever be in this life," Vega said.

Manny shrugged off the insult, as if it didn't matter.

A car drove up and a bunch of Anglo girls got out with bags of food. They wore thin, tight dresses and high, fancy boots. They laid the bags down under the sycamore and got back into the car without saying a word. But as they drove off all the girls held up two fingers in the peace sign.

The sun was pouring down now on the vines out of a hard, blue sky. It warmed the grapes and they gave off a sweet, musky smell.

Then, somewhere up by the winery, a motor started up. It was a big motor, running slow and deep-throated. We listened to it but said nothing.

A car full of sheriffs stopped on the road and one of them jumped out, carrying a shotgun over his arm. He was clean-faced and wore well-pressed khakis and a short-sleeved shirt.

"Hi," he said to me in a voice that he meant to be pleasant but wasn't. "What's going on? Not agitating, are you?"

"Just talking," I said.

"Who are you?" he said.

I took my wallet out and showed him my badge. He gave it a long, hard look as if he didn't believe me, mumbled something, and got back in the car. The car went down the road very slowly, with the shotguns sticking out the windows so everyone could see them.

The vineyard ran for about half a mile along the main road and it sloped up toward the hill where the winery sat. The rows were set out at right angles to the road, so when you looked at them they ran up and away from you, as straight as railroad tracks.

The sound of the deep-throated motor faded away now. You couldn't hear it clearly because of the crowd of workers and their wives and children clustered around the barrier. They were beginning to chant a prayer of some kind.

The picker came into sight over the brow of the hill, below the winery. It was headed down the first row of vines. It seemed to be walking along, not running on wheels. Then, as it came closer, you could see the big wheels move. You could see the red body straddling the

207

row of grape vines and the yellow canopy with a man sitting under it, out of the hot sun.

The chanting of the crowd grew louder and then suddenly broke up into shouts.

Manny called over to Arturo Vega who was still sitting with his guitar under the tree. "Give us the one about Pancho. The one where he takes his cannons apart and loads them on burros and marches his men across the Guadalupes and down to Agua Prieta."

"I don't know that one so good," Vega called back.

"Play it anyway," Manny said. "And make it sweet. But make it soft and sad when the *soldados* beat Pancho and his men on the mesa at the gates of Prieta."

The grape picker came closer. You couldn't hear the motor now, only the sound of the machinery. A cloud of thin green dust billowed around it.

"I'm going across the road," Manny said. "Hold the fort, Mr. Delaney. Will you?"

"I'll hold it," I said, although I wasn't sure what he meant.

He was smiling and there was a far-off, questing look in his eyes as if he were on his way to meet Coronado and Captain Cortez.

The machine was near the main road now. It had wide arms with steel, fingerlike rods that reached down and gathered in leaves and small branches and grape clusters, everything. Then the steel fingers shook everything hard that it had gathered in, like a terrier shaking a rat, and dumped it into a big hopper.

Manny ran across the road, loping his pigeon-toed run, the way he had run across the bullring in Tijuana. Where the row of grape vines ended, he stood in front of the big red machine that was coming slowly down the row.

The crowd at the barrier stopped their chanting. It was quiet except for the clank of the machine and Vega's guitar twanging away under the sycamore tree.

Then Manny knelt with his hands at his sides and his chin raised, defying the machine as he had defied the bull. A woman screamed. A voice shouted a hoarse word of warning and I realized that it was my own voice I had heard.

There was another scream as I ran across the road. The ditch beside the road was wider than it looked. I fell and heard shouts and the sound of running feet. I struggled up and ducked under the barbed wire fence.

Thunderheads were building up. The air was still and hot and smelled of electricity.

The red machine had reached the end of the row. Manuel was still on his knees, his hands stiff at his sides and his face lifted defiantly. I don't know whether the driver sitting under his yellow canopy saw him or not. I don't think it would have made any difference one way or the other.

The machine came lumbering on and the boy knelt there defying it. He didn't move. Then the steel fingers reached out and, as if it was harvesting grapes, picked flesh from bone and gathered him in.

33

Lambert's paper ran a big story the next morning about the events at La Cresta Vineyard. There was a picture of workers running across a field, men with their fists raised, women with their hair streaming out behind. The picture must have been taken just as the red machine came to a halt, just before the sheriffs with the shotguns rushed in to quiet the crowd.

The story told how two squads of sheriffs had prevented a riot without so much as firing a shot. It spoke about the great success of the mechanical picker that had harvested the whole La Cresta Vineyard in less time than it would take a hundred men. The story also told about the death of Manuel Castillo, a young agitator, who had been killed when he was blinded by the sun and wandered in front of the grape picker.

Later that morning Chief Barton called me at the office and congratulated me on keeping the gangs out of the trouble at La Cresta. Then he told me that Lieutenant Simpson had quit the force and taken a position up north in Sonoma.

"Would you like his job?" Chief Barton asked me. "It pays two thousand more than you're making."

I made up my mind right there on the phone, but I told him I wanted to talk to my wife before deciding. That night I asked Alice what she thought about the offer.

"Isn't it better," she said, "to keep people from being arrested than it is to spend your time arresting people?"

Next morning I told Chief Barton that I was going to stay with parole work. But it made me feel good that he had confidence in me again. And it helped me to forget the time up in Bakersfield when Harold Jensen jumped out the window and left me holding a pair of empty handcuffs.

We had a service for Manuel out at Los Tres Gavilanes Rojos on the following Sunday. All the gangs showed up and there was a lot of music and corn tortillas and red frijoles. Arturo Vega played his guitar and everyone sang the rebel song about Zapata and the sad, gay song about Pancho Villa that Manuel liked. It was a good time altogether. Down here on the border, death is a faithful and true companion.

It's been more than a month now since the events at La Cresta. But the town is still talking about them and Vega has written a corrido about them and about Manuel Castillo. It's not a very good corrido but I wouldn't be surprised if it's around for a long, long time.